# WRAPPING PAPER RIVALS

## THERESA HALVORSEN

Copyright © 2024 by Theresa Halvorsen

All rights reserved.

No part of this book may be reproduced in any form or by any electronic or mechanical means, including information storage and retrieval systems, without written permission from the author, except for the use of brief quotations in a book review.

The story, all names, characters and incidents portrayed in this production are fictitious. No identification with actual persons (living or deceased), places and buildings is intended or should be inferred.

ISBN Ebook: 978-1-955431-24-8

ISBN Paperback: 978-1-955431-25-5

For information about special discounts available for bulk purchases contact www.nobadbookspress.com

*To my mother,*
*for sharing her love of dolls*

# CHAPTER 1

The Nutcracker Suite began playing over my store's speakers, and I raised my hand, pretending to conduct an orchestra as musical chimes sounded throughout the famous Christmas piece. Caught in the moment, I closed my eyes, taking a break from all the Christmas chaos to enjoy myself. I would have to do the math, but I was betting today, the day after Thanksgiving, was my highest sale day ever.

The beautiful orchestra music cut off, and Mariah Carey at full volume, belted from the speakers, rattling my store's windows. My eyes flew open.

"Stop playing," I snapped to my voice-activated sound system. The music stopped. "Really, Charles? Mariah Carey?"

There was no answer, which was probably a good thing. My ghost had only communicated with me by messing with the store's electrical system, adding cold spots in random places, and knocking merchandise over. If he? She? Started talking, I'd have a heart attack. I'd named him Charles, though I had no idea if the name was even close to his given one.

"Play the Nutcracker Suite," I asked my sound system, ignoring the sudden drop in temperature. I tried to get back into the Christmas zone—the celebratory feel and anticipation of the next month of Christmas joy—but the perfect moment was gone. Oh well, it would be back. And I should focus, instead of orchestrating an imaginary band. I'd sent my assistant Franklin home to enjoy Thanksgiving leftovers with his friends and was looking forward to a peaceful evening. Eyeing my shop, I gauged I had about thirty more minutes of work. Perfect time to order some to-go food, so it'd be ready when I was done with my day. I didn't have the energy to cook tonight, and the rest of this weekend was going to be crazy. The leftovers would be gold.

Mariah Carey started playing again, and I unplugged the system. "Enough! We've listened to that song four times today. No more. In fact, no more Christmas music." I doubted Charles would listen to me, so I popped in earbuds to listen to some Taylor Swift (yep—I'm one of those middle-aged Swifties). Humming to myself, I started closing my doll shop, restocking the specialty Barbies, the furniture kits for dollhouses, and the multitude of tiny doll clothes and even tinier little shoes. My store did well with dollhouse and miniature furniture accessories, and I restocked a few empty areas; I'd have to place another order sooner than expected. I finished by tidying up the doll parts area, a spot hidden behind a screen after a TikTok someone recorded in my store got several hundreds of thousands of views for all the doll parts in their bins. It wasn't surprising dolls creeped some people out, but I hadn't expected the horrified comments because of the different sized arms, legs, wigs, and eyeballs all carefully organized for doll makers to find. The

TikTok had boosted my on-line sales, which was a bonus, but after that I now hid the parts behind a screen where customers didn't HAVE to see them.

Valuable Barbies, exclusive and hard to find Monster Highs from comic-book conventions and special edition Madame Alexanders sat behind glass cases, and I scrubbed away the fingerprints of those who had gotten a little close. I rearranged the paper ornaments on the giant holiday tree in the middle of the store. I loved setting up a Giving Tree every year, where shoppers could pick a handwritten ornament for a foster child and purchase the gifts for them, returning the presents to my store for me to pass out at a huge Christmas dinner in a few weeks. As a foster child, I remembered the one year I'd gotten gifts under the tree—clean socks, new jeans that fit and a simple fashion doll. I spent the next few months doing odd jobs so I could purchase different outfits for her.

My next round of foster parents had taken that doll away when I'd forgotten to unload the dishwasher, caught up in a homework assignment. I'd never seen her again, and within a few weeks, was sent to another foster home.

Shoving away the memories, I ran a compressed air can through the dollhouses, blowing away any stray dust over the furnishings and straightening the Christmas decorations I'd hung within.

A rattle at the front door caught my attention. I turned around and shouted a "sorry, closed!" to the woman who'd cupped her eyes to see within the store. Knowing if I paid any attention she'd keep knocking or pleading to be let in, I turned my back and kept on dusting. I had a firm rule about reopening after I was closed—even during Christmas. If I stayed too late, I wouldn't get any rest. And I was starving and couldn't wait to get my feet up, drink a cold glass of white wine and enjoy fiery curry while watching some cheesy Christmas romance. This was my favorite time of the year, and I was going to enjoy every cliché.

I startled when the silver bell I'd hung over the door handle started jangling.

"Charles, stop it," I hissed, hunching my back and resisting the urge to turn around and see if the woman was still there. "I'm closed and I'm not opening that door." But he ignored me and kept jangling the bell, the sound echoing through the store. After a minute or two of the non-stop noise, I spun around with a frustrated sigh. A haunted doll shop sounded amazing in theory, but in practicality, it was a pain in the ass.

The woman, bundled in a blue beanie and holiday scarf, her red hair attractively framing her face, was still at the door, typing frantically on her phone. I'd always envied women who were natural redheads. My hair was black and had luckily resisted graying as it also resisted coloring. I wore it in a short multi-layered bob that highlighted my narrow nose and big blue eyes.

Charles rang the silver bell so loudly it echoed into the street, making the woman look up from her phone. Our eyes met through the window, and she smiled happily.

Swell. She'd gotten my attention.

I stomped to the door, reminding myself as I flung it open that I wasn't actually mad at her. "I'm sorry, we're closed." I worked to keep my voice modulated and friendly, though firm.

"I know, and I'm a horrible person. It's my niece's birthday, we're celebrating over at the restaurant Serenity, in fact everyone is already there, and my stupid brother, not my niece's parent—by the way—didn't get her a present, even though he said he was going to. And I'm sorry, and I suck, and I know you're closed, and I'll pay double, or triple or whatever, but she loves your store and has one of the Fashion Dream Dolls, or has a bunch, or something and I wanted to get her some clothes for it, and this is terrible of me—"

I stopped the woman before she'd faint from lack of oxygen. "I'm so sorry, but—"

"Please. It's been a really rough year for my family. They all came in for Thanksgiving, and it's been ... bumpy. I'm hoping if we can get through my niece's birthday dinner, we'll get past it."

The door I was holding partially open, so my body blocked it, was wrenched from my hand, flinging wide as Charles decided I was going to help this woman out.

"Come on in," I said with a sigh. "I actually just got in some great clothes for the Fashion Dreams for the holiday. Knee-high boots, a cute little hoodie that has cat ears, and this embroidered bohemian shirt. They're selling like mad, and I can barely keep them stocked."

"Oh, thank you, thank you, thank you. I'm Lara, by the way."

"Kayla." I led the woman over to the selection of doll clothes, but stopped when Lara paused. She stared around her, open-mouthed. "This is the coolest thing I've ever seen."

# CHAPTER 2

*J*turned around to see whatever had distracted Lara. I desperately wanted to go home and didn't want to get into a long conversation. She needed to buy her gifts and head to her niece's birthday celebration. "What's cool?" I asked, trying to be patient.

"Your store."

"Oh. Thank you." My irritation melted a bit, and I took a second to look around, trying to see my business how Lara saw it.

Five years ago, when I'd opened Enchanted Kingdom Toys, I'd installed a giant-colored glass chandelier that cast gentle shades of pink, blue, purple, green, and yellow over everything. After doing careful research, I'd stayed away from the formal, elegant, and sterile atmosphere of other doll shops and had laid down polished cement floors with turquoise and violet glitter in patterns that looked like flowing streams. I'd painted the brick walls with bright murals of families, giant flowers, mythological creatures, and trees. My store had high ceilings with a circling wrought iron staircase that led up to an unused office on the second floor. A balcony off the office overlooked the store. I decorated the steps of the staircase and balcony for each season and this holiday I'd filled them with various bright packages and doll accoutrements, along with twinkle lights, tinsel, and wrapping paper over everything. I even scented my store with a mixture of cinnamon and cypress trees to really hammer home the Christmas point.

I'd been very lucky to get this store in the "old" (i.e. tourist) part of town, on the main street. Hotels hemmed in each side of the five blocks of Old Towne (the E is important—never forget the E!) and the street was peppered with restaurants and interesting stores. The city invested a lot of money in the aesthetics of our area, especially around Christmas time, and people came from hundreds of miles for their holiday fun. I knew my doll store wouldn't be as prosperous in a different town. I owed the city council a hundred times over for helping my dream of owning a toy store be successful.

"I can see why people adore this place," Lara continued. "This store is on all the tourist sites and my niece always asks to come here. In fact, we were supposed to come today, but there was family drama."

"I'm sorry. What's that saying: you can pick your friends, but not your family?"

Lara grimaced a bit. "Yeah, and ours is complex. My brother and I actually tried not to pick them, but that's another story. And one my niece isn't responsible for. So I'm not punishing her. Every child should get spoiled on their birthday and at Christmas time."

"My sentiment exactly," I said, warming to this woman, despite my annoyance at reopening the store for her. "Come on, let's get your niece her present."

Lara exclaimed over the doll clothes for the Fashion Dream Dolls, finally selecting the green hoodie with the cat ears, a mini-skirt and a pair of patterned knee-high boots, all completely matching and would look super cute on the doll. She took her purchases over to the counter for me to ring up and wandered over to the glass shelves to inspect the more valuable dolls.

"I had one of these Barbies." She pointed to a doll with big blonde hair and a frilly pink top, still in her original and undamaged box.

"A Pink Jubilee Barbie!" I said. "Those are pretty valuable if in box and unplayed with."

Lara chuckled. "Then mine's not worth anything. I played with her, took off her clothes, brushed her hair. Then eventually, she ended up taking baths with me. She loved every moment," she said with a wink. "I still have her somewhere."

"That's what you're supposed to do with dolls. And everyone played with the Pink Jubilee Barbie, since you could create a bunch of different outfits with what was in the box. No one kept her in mint condition and that's what makes her so crazy rare."

"Got her on Christmas morning," Lara mused. "I think I was seven and still convinced Santa existed. I was so excited he got me what I wanted."

"Those are the best memories," I said, scanning the price tags on the doll clothes. "When you rip open the paper on a present, see a hint of what's inside and can't wait to get the rest of the paper off, you're so eager."

Lara's face got that nostalgic glitter so many adults got when they remembered the joy of Christmas morning. When they remembered that someone cared enough to get them presents under the tree, sit with them, and watch them unwrap the presents. I knew it wasn't always perfect for a lot of families. Hell, my Christmases were always horrible. But I enjoyed bringing up the memories for others and giving them the echo of the joy they'd felt.

"Do you want me to wrap this up? I still have some non-Christmas wrapping paper and it's free. One of our perks," I said.

"Oh yes, please." Lara visibly shook off the memories. "My brother's store offers gift wrapping too, but he charges for it and it's just some random high schooler who does a terrible job. I'm sure you'll do better. Oh, I'm going to take one of these too." Lara took a paper ornament off the Giving Tree and distracted me from asking more about her brother's shop. "This is sweet," she said, reading the ornament. "This kid wants a coloring book, a storybook about dragons and five pairs of socks. Oddly specific, but totally doable. Do I bring them back here?"

"Yes please. Unwrapped. I work with a local foster organization, and we make sure these kids get the presents they asked for." I focused on wrapping each item of doll clothes in a different color of paper—glittery purples, greens, and blues, ensuring there was no hint of Christmas in the wrapping. Then I tied them together with a giant silvery ribbon. "What's your niece's name? I'll put her name on the outside of a card, and you can fill in the inside with whatever message you want."

"It's Sage. You're my new hero," Lara said. "Between opening back up for me, helping me choose a present for my niece, and now helping foster kids." She chose another ornament. "I'm going to help this kid, too. I mean, you hear such horror stories about kids who every morning collect their things in a trash bag and put it by the front door because they don't think they'll end up staying with their family. And the abuse and neglect and..."

The memory of my own belongings, one pair of shoes, one set of jeans, a beloved copy of the Wizard of Oz, and a ripped-up sweatshirt thrown into a trash bag and flung into the front yard for my social worker to grab, punched through me and I had to breathe to push the memory away.

Lara kept prattling away, detailing the horrible stories she'd heard on the news, unaware she'd triggered my memories.

"It is hard to be a foster kid," I said, interrupting her and forcing my thoughts down. "That's why I'm proud to offer the tree. We take the presents until the foster kids' dinner on the 21st. Your total is $52.53. Cash or card?"

"Oh, card," Lara said with a laugh. "I don't think anyone has extra cash this time of year." She pulled out her card and ran it through the swiper. I wondered how cold my dinner would be by the time I got to it. Well, it didn't matter; microwaved Thai food was still pretty good. I passed her the gifts just as my front door flew open.

"Why did you come here? I told you I'd take care of it!"

## CHAPTER 3

I yelped. How could I have forgotten to lock the front door? I slid my finger down to the panic button installed under the cash register, ready to summon the cops if I needed to.

The man at the front door wore a green flannel shirt and no hat or gloves. Snowflakes freckled his hair, and his muscular frame filled the doorway. A car idled in an empty parking spot in front of the store, headlights still on. He pointed at Lara. "Come on, sis! I told you I had stuff at my store Sage would've liked. I was just going back to get it. You didn't need to come here." An icy wind blew into the store from the open door, riffling the paper ornaments on the tree.

Lara turned, her hands on her hips. "Yeah, moron. But Sage loves this store. And when you'd texted, you said you were already at the restaurant and forgot to pick something up for her. I decided to take care of the problem and get her a present she'd love. That way, it didn't look like you'd forgotten, and you didn't have to leave the Party-of-Sucks."

Party-of-Sucks? What the hell? I took my finger off the panic button. They were obviously siblings, and I was stuck in the middle of some family drama.

Swell. Perfect end to my crazy day.

"I didn't forget," the man said, continuing to argue. "I just—"

"Got busy," Lara said. "Yeah, we're aware."

"It's the day after Thanksgiving! It's one of the busiest days for me."

"I know," Lara said, a little gentler. "No one is upset about that."

"And Dylan always—"

"He's a jerk," Lara said. "Come in out of the cold; I'm almost done."

As the store lights illuminated his face, I recognized this giant man with his blonde hair falling over his glasses; Patrick Graves, the owner of a general toy store a few blocks over. He sold Legos, board games, and small touristy junk that broke after a few uses. I'd barely been in his store, but as I recalled, it was boring and lacked the imagination most toy stores had. He'd displayed boxes of toys on wire racks that were kind-of organized by type. Prices were marked using label maker tape and dusty signs stated some items were on "sale." There was no whimsy or color or fun anywhere in his store. He didn't even have display toys for the kids to play with and fall in love with, forcing the parent into a sale, or risk a tantrum. I'd met him at a few networking meetings the city council had put on, but he'd seemed as boring as his store; almost like he was at the meeting for the free donuts and coffee. He was Lara's brother? I didn't know this woman, but she seemed like the complete opposite of him.

He was good-looking though, with high cheekbones, full lips, and pale green eyes, the glasses adding just the right amount of character to keep him from being too handsome. Maybe his looks contributed to his success—I envisioned single moms flocking to his store, batting their eyelashes and offering to sweep his floor, like some sort of crazy groupies. I shook my head and pushed away the image; I really needed to eat something.

"We're going to be late." Patrick pulled out his phone and swiped at the screen. "Sister-Long-Hair keeps bugging, which you'd know if you checked your phone."

Lara pulled out her phone and winced at the messages. "God, that woman needs to find another ex-husband."

I raised an eyebrow. Wow, sounded like the drama in this family was pretty epic. Normally, I'd be trying to get the details; Lara seemed like the over-share type. But I was too tired and hungry to really care. "It's a good thing you're all done," I told Lara, handing her the wrapped packages. There was literally a container of spicy curry with my name on it. "Enjoy your evening, both of you."

"This is the most amazing store. I got the cutest things here," Lara said, verbally poking at her brother. "They're so much cuter than the stuff you sell. And Sage is going to love them, which is the important part."

Got it. I was awesome; her brother was a bit of an ass and I just wanted to go home. I was tempted to shoo them out like I would a stray dog. *Go on! Get with ya! Go home!*

"And you probably paid more than you should've," Patrick murmured, somehow not receiving my telepathic wish for him to leave. His eyes swept around my store, taking in the multi-colored chandelier, the murals, the balcony full of wrapped presents and all the merchandise cleverly displayed to be elegant and yet whimsical. Maybe I should offer to teach him how to create a toy store that maximized fun with profit.

Or not. His store was only two years old and if he was still stacking boxes on wire racks, he wouldn't be in business much longer, anyway. The storefront he was in had gone through several iterations and owners in the five years since I'd opened Enchanted Kingdom Toys. It would likely go through some more. Probably a specialty boutique next.

"Sage will love the presents momentarily," Patrick said, forcing his eyes away from the chandelier and back to his sister. "She'll play with them for thirty seconds, then get distracted and forget all about them. Toys are disposable and whatever you bought, and probably overpaid for, is no different."

"Excuse me?" I said, annoyance melting my desire to go home. My cheeks warmed. "I strongly disagree. Haven't you ever seen a toddler become hysterical because their stuffed animal got lost or damaged? Ever seen a child who can't sleep because their favorite toy got left at Grandma's house? Toys aren't disposable. Not to the children who love them. Or at least, not the toys I sell."

"I get what you're going for here." Patrick bent his head to look into a modern dollhouse display. "But dolls and dollhouses and all of this are on their way out. Especially with modern parents. Dolls teach girls their value is in being mothers, being domestic. Parents want their daughters to have careers, be empowered. Dolls don't enforce that message. I've been listening to this podcast about it." He pulled out his phone, his fingers swiping, unaware my hands shook with anger. "You'll have to pivot your store in a few years, diversify, or you'll go out of business."

"I so phenomenally disagree," I snapped. "Dolls teach empathy, allow children to act out various events, and imagine social situations and how to deal with them. I don't care what your podcast says. Podcast hosts aren't experts. They're just idiots trying to get monetized."

"Actually podcasts—" Patrick tried to interrupt, but I was on a roll.

"Dolls teach imagination, which in our current corporate environment—I also listen to podcasts by the way—is missing in many modern adults," I said, mocking his use of the word modern. "If you ever watched a child playing with a doll, you'd see the depth of their imagination. Watch them build homes, fight off dinosaur attacks and, yes, dress up in different outfits, which helps them build personality and personas. And girls aren't the only ones who enjoy playing with dolls." I was actually doing pretty well with a collection of dolls for boys. They weren't a top seller, but they did well with online orders.

"But you're just fighting against the screens," Patrick continued, pushing his glasses up his nose. "Parents want to keep their kids quiet so they hand tablets with various games to their kids, so the kids shut up. The restaurant we're heading to is going to be full of kids on screens. Heck Sage will open her present and then not play with her new toys, but with a screen. The key to a successful toy store is selling cheap toys to make the parents give their kid a gift at Christmas or holidays, so the kids can unwrap, exclaim and then forget about it. Dolls are expensive and just don't sell."

Why was this man selling toys? I'd never met the owner of a toy store who didn't love the joy and imagination toys brought.

"Dolls don't sell in your store because of her." Lara tugged on her lip. "I'm thinking she has the market cornered on dolls in this town. Besides, it doesn't sound like you like dolls, anyway."

"I don't," Patrick said and glanced at his phone, which had

continued to buzz. "Look, we gotta go. Sister-Long-Hair says they're going to order without us and that means she's going to insist the rest of the family not eat their food until our order gets delivered. And that's going to suck for everyone."

Lara groaned. "I really dislike her."

"Join the club." He turned to me. "Fun debate. That podcast is Growth Gurus if you want to give it a listen. It'll change your entire business model. You have to diversify. All of this is going obsolete."

I raised an eyebrow. He was giving ME advice on how to run a toy store? Mr-just-throw-the-toys-onto-a-shelf-and-hope-someone-would-buy-them? I doubted he'd still be in business after Christmas.

"And how is my livelihood going obsolete?"

"I don't mean that dolls are going to be obsolete. All toys are going to be. We're at the tail-end of the rush." He stumbled a bit and rubbed at an arm. The chandelier over our heads tinkled, the bits of colored glass rubbing against each other. Charles had taken offense at what Patrick was saying. Why had the stupid ghost made me open the door, anyway?

"Is that a general business podcast?" I asked. "Or an owning a toy store podcast? Because I've never heard any of this."

"These guys are geniuses. They've helped a ton of new businesses turn profitable within the first six months of opening. I'm telling you because there's a way out. But if you don't pivot, you're going to be out of business."

"Interesting," I said. "I'll tell you what. I'll check them out, if you check out mine, Toy Shop Chronicles. It's actually for toy stores and I bet it says a lot of different stuff than that bro one you listen to."

"They're not bros. They're—" he trailed off. "Okay, they

kind-of are bros. I never noticed." He pursed his lips. "Good point. I'll check yours. Can't do any harm."

Oh. Okay then. I felt oddly deflated, the exhaustion flooding back in now that we weren't arguing anymore.

"Thank you for your purchase," I said to Lara. "I hope Sage enjoys her gifts." I was done and couldn't wait to pick up my takeout, get off my feet and enjoy an enormous glass of wine. Maybe two. I'd earned it.

"Thank you." Lara collected the presents and reached across the counter to squeeze my fingers. "Ignore him. I think you have a wonderful store and can see why everyone wants to come here."

"And I need to lock up." Circling to the front of the counter, I put my hand on the small of Lara's back, and gently nudged her to the front door, opening it and letting in the chilly breeze. They stepped out, and I locked it behind her and her brother with a snick.

Time to go home. There was just one more thing I had to do.

## CHAPTER 4

"Here kitty, kitty, kitty," I called into the back alley behind my store. The back door where I accepted supplies and—during the COVID shut-down, had passed merchandise through—was open, letting a patch of warm yellow light onto the cobblestone street. I stood in the middle of the alley, the cat's bowl in one hand, an open can of cat food in the other.

"Come on, kitty," I yelled into the frosty night.

No response.

I searched the shadows with my phone's flashlight, hoping for a telltale sign of movement or the glitter of eyes.

Nothing.

I clinked on the can of wet food with my fingernail, hoping the clink of the metal would bring the black cat out.

"Max? Here kitty, kitty." I had no idea if Max was the cat's name or not, but it was what I'd named it. I'd spotted the cat about three months ago, riffling around in a dumpster. It hadn't let me get close, but when I'd put out a bowl of cat food before leaving in the evenings, I'd come back to find it licked clean.

Over the next few weeks, I kept feeding the cat, though I almost never saw him; just kept coming back to clean bowls in the alley. Then, one day as I'd set out the bowl, Max had crept out from under a dumpster, and had let me watch him eat between growls warning me away, then had bolted when I'd tried to take a step toward him. It took a few weeks, but soon he'd come running when I opened the door and would eat without growling at me. At two months into our relationship, he allowed me to stroke his back. Then he started sticking around after he finished eating, rubbing against my legs, purring and letting me pet him. Last week he'd let me scoop him up and had head-butted me until he curled into my arms, purring like a motorcycle. Eventually, he'd hopped down and bolted, but we were making progress. I wanted to take him to the vet, get him some shots, see if he needed to be neutered, but one step at a time. For now, I was just happy to have a friend with boundaries.

But tonight, Max didn't come, no matter how many times I called and banged the can on his bowl. He'd been getting bigger, thicker around the middle; maybe he'd gotten adopted, or another store owner had let him stay safe from the cold. I tightened my jacket around my arms as the winter wind made me shiver.

I tried one last time. "Max? Here kitty!"

God, I hoped a car or something hadn't hit him. Patrick and Lara had delayed me, and I'd been later than normal; maybe Max had given up on me and gone to wherever he went in the evenings. I dumped the food into his dish and set it on the ground. Hopefully, I'd come back in the morning and find it licked clean, like in the old days. I went back inside my store, closing the back door behind me and looked down at the puffy cat bed I'd just purchased. My goal tonight had been to get Max inside out of the cold, but I guess it wasn't going to happen. Not tonight, at least.

Feeling a bit melancholy, I turned out the store's lights, leaving the Christmas lights going as a security measure. With my keys in hand, I opened the front door and engaged the security alarm.

"Good night, Charles," I called, as I always did. It felt rude to just leave him without some sort of acknowledgement, though it wasn't like he returned the favor most nights.

But tonight, as if in response, a teddy bear dropped from the balcony to the floor. "You'd better pick that up," I said, though I doubted it would happen. I'd have to come back in the morning and return the bear to its place.

I drove to the Thai restaurant, picking up my cold takeout and getting a lecture from the owner about how they'd kept the restaurant open waiting for me. Hell, today had been rough.

Unlocking the front door of my seventy-five-year-old craftsman, I kicked off my shoes with a groan. I loved owning a toy store during the holidays, but the twelve-plus hours on my feet were getting harder as I got older. Heading into the kitchen, I stuck my food in the microwave and uncorked a bottle of white wine.

The microwave chimed at the same time my phone vibrated. I looked at the screen and swiped up to talk. "Luke!" I said. "Everything okay? You don't usually call this late." It was pushing nine o'clock.

"I just have some news," my son said. "Didn't want it to wait until morning."

## CHAPTER 5

"What happened?" I asked Luke. "Are you okay? Is Ivy okay?" I asked, making sure nothing had happened to my step-granddaughter.

"I'm sorry," Luke said. "I said it wrong. Yes, everyone is fine. Didn't mean to scare you. Ivy is fine, and so is Tara."

"Oh, thank God," I said. I pulled my chicken curry out of the microwave and speared a piece of carrot, popping it into my mouth. "What's going on?" I breathed out the heat of the microwaved carrot combined with the spicy of the curry.

He took a deep breath. "I'm pretty sure I'm going to get Christmas off. My boss said I could probably get it, but he didn't want to promise yet. But he said I could get plane tickets, but to make sure they were refundable, just in case."

Hmmm … I wasn't liking this hedging. "So … you're coming back for Christmas?"

"That's the plan. I think my boss just wants to make sure he's being fair to everyone and I'm so new."

"Oh good," I said. I'd been so looking forward to seeing him and his new family and having a little girl around for

Christmas morning. Luke married Tara a little over a year ago, adopting her eight-year-old daughter at the same time. It had been a bit of a whirlwind wedding, with Luke only being twenty-two, compared to Tara's thirty-four, but they seemed to be making it work. And it wasn't like I'd figured out the whole marriage and children thing. I'd had Luke when I was eighteen, thinking I knew what I was doing and had never gotten married.

Hell, I still didn't know what I was doing.

"So, what can I get Tara for Christmas? Ivy, I'm sure I can figure something out."

"Ummm, mom, Ivy doesn't like dolls. I know you'd love to get her a giant dollhouse, but she wouldn't appreciate it."

I took another bite of my dinner. "I know," I said, though he was right, and I was dying to get her a dollhouse she could retrofit into her own fun. But just because I wanted to give her something, didn't mean she actually wanted it. "She's a total science nerd, and I was thinking of a telescope. Sound good?"

I could hear the smile in his voice. "She would love that."

"Oh good. I think there are apps she can use too, so she can use that to figure out what she's looking at. And what about Tara? And you? What do you want?"

We discussed various gifts, the conversation naturally segueing as we talked about Ivy, Tara, and then his new job for a few minutes before he had to get off the phone to start dinner for his family. He was in Arizona, and I was in Connecticut, so it was barely six there. Pouring another half-glass of wine in celebration, I toasted the air. I'd been dreading the idea that Luke wouldn't be able to get time off for Christmas and I'd have to spend the holiday all alone. I stared out my kitchen window where I could see the neighbor's holiday light display—white twinkle lights in their trees and around their eaves. Snow began to fall, turning the view into something magical.

And clichéd.

I pushed the thought away. That was a dangerous thought for a toy shop owner to have at Christmas time. I needed to lean into every cliché to keep my business afloat.

Having finished my wine, I made a cup of chamomile tea and took it to my desk. My house was so tiny, I'd had to set up my desk in a corner of the bedroom, but it was simply a space for a computer with a comfortable chair. A few years ago, I'd taken the time to replace my dated and dark bedroom furniture with pale cream furnishings and seagrass and sage colored bedding. The rug I'd placed over the original hardwood floors reminded me of the forest, with its leaf pattern echoed in the cozy quilt I'd found at an antique store. Prints of trees, trunks, and leaves finished the room, creating a restful space I could retreat to.

I mean, I didn't know who I was retreating from, since few came to visit me, but the idea was there. It was unfortunate it was the only spot my desk computer fit in, as sometimes working from home only increased my stress and destroyed the Zen feeling of the room. But the desk literally wouldn't fit anywhere else.

I snapped the blinds closed on the holiday display from another neighbor, whose teenagers had decorated the house with the attitude of the-more-lights-the-better, regardless of whether it went together. I loved the joy of the display, but tonight I was tired and needed to focus.

Taking a sip of tea, I logged onto my store's online order website. Online orders for dolls, their outfits, miniature accessories, and even orders for some of the doll parts were pouring in. My jaw dropped. I'd had twenty-two orders since this morning. I didn't think I'd ever had that much in a single day. Besides my store sales, this was definitely shaping up to be the best Black Friday I'd ever had. I'd have to go in early in the morning to get the orders ready for shipping.

I loved the extra revenue from online orders, but this time of year, the amount of work they created could be overwhelming, not to mention dealing with the returns and packages that never made it to their location. If this was going to continue, Franklin and I may need a different system. While he was the best thing I'd ever invested in, he could lack attention to detail and I'd caught him getting so caught up chatting with customers, he'd forgotten to ring people up and had simply sent them on their way, with their purchases in hand. Maybe I'd have him package up the online orders while I worked with the shoppers trying to find that perfect gift. Though he was better at upselling on the doll accessories, long as he remembered to charge people. And last week he'd even sold three of the Barbies and two of the Madame Alexander's from the rare doll case.

I clicked over to the store's email, skimming through the inquiries and starting to reply. Many were questions about our holiday hours, which were posted on the website, requests for special orders or questions if we had something specific in stock. My favorite was the one asking if we sold Thomas the Train. Normally, I'd have pointed the person toward Patrick's store, but I wouldn't be doing that ever again. That man had no business being in toy sales. So, I simply responded that we didn't and apologized. They could find what they needed online, probably.

I answered a few more emails, falling into the routine of completing tasks. I'd just finished sending over the pictures I had saved on my computer detailing a Madame Alexander 1960s bride doll when my phone buzzed.

> We have a problem.

It was my friend Daphne from the city council who, among other things, planned the holiday dinner and gift exchange for the community's foster kids. Oh hell, it was nearly ten o'clock; way too late for most people to be reaching out. And Daphne was an early to bed, early to rise for her five a.m. workout with her personal trainer kind of girl. I should wait to respond until the morning and not get sucked into whatever was going on.

My phone buzzed again.

> Still awake? I could use some help on this. Kind of freaking out.

Whelp, that wasn't like Daphne; she'd always seemed like she could handle anything.

> What kind of problem?

> Oh thank God, you're still awake. Jeffrey, who was in charge of the foster kids' dinner.

The message stopped there, though the three dots showing she was still typing went on for a little while and I stared at my phone, frustration growing. What the hell was going on?

> Jeffrey fell down his front stairs, and it's pretty bad. His doctor pulled him from working for the rest of December. He's going to need to surgery on his ankle and can't work for the rest of December.

> Oh no.

I vaguely remembered the tall steps leading from the sidewalk up to Jeffrey's front door—during the winter, those could be dangerous.

> I think he lives on the street behind me or two over. Want me to check on him or take him some food? I can leave it on his doorstep, so he doesn't have to get up.

That's a good idea.

> I bet his wife would appreciate the help. But the problem is the dinner for the foster kids. Jeffrey was in charge of it! Like, in charge, in charge of it. Like I don't know where the planning is at, who the caterer is, who has agreed to donate toys. I know NOTHING.

Okay, this was pretty bad, and I understood Daphne's stress, but Jeffrey was super organized and always pulled off the event. He probably had all the pieces in place. She just had to find his notes and emails. She should totally have access to all of that.

> It's three weeks away. Should be okay.

Jeffrey hasn't done anything.

> Wait, what? What do you mean anything?

> There's NOTHING planned. He didn't even book a caterer. The lists of the kids and their requests are in a gigantic pile of sticky notes on his desk. We can't read half of it. We need Christmas trees, someone to organize the presents and make sure each kid gets a present—ideally the presents they asked for —we need desserts, caterers, invitations, RSVPs.

I could visualize Daphne, her curly black hair spiraling around her face, as she sat in her office in the darkened city hall, staring at an empty checklist. Would we even have the dinner? Would the kids get their gifts? I knew my store was collecting donations at least, and I knew other businesses were, too. But if there was no dinner, how would we get them to the kids in time for Christmas? Deliver them to each house on Christmas Eve like Santa would? I shook my head. That was ridiculous. There were three weeks before the dinner. We could pull something together.

> How can he have done nothing? That's not like him. This is his sixth time planning it. These poor kids.

> He's had the flu since early November. Now this fall.

> That's terrible.

My teacup was empty, and this conversation made me want more wine.

> I hate to ask, but I know how much supporting foster kids means to you. Do you have time to help? I'm calling a planning meeting of everyone I can get tomorrow at two. Can I put you in charge?

Um, actually no, she couldn't. I owned a toy store. A toy store at Christmas time. This was an insane ask.

> I know you're probably freaking out. But no one else would care about these kids the way you would.

This was insane. I couldn't be in charge of the entire party. There were seventy-five kids on the list, last I heard. Coordinating that many gifts, combined with a dinner for them and their families or group homes, would be overwhelming. Especially if Daphne didn't even have a caterer. But for many, especially the ones in group homes, this would be their only holiday present, their only real celebration. I knew what it was like to get nothing for Christmas. To be ignored by your foster family because you weren't actually a part of the "real family." And to know the money that was supposed to be for me from the state had gone to buy my "siblings" a new iPad and Xbox, I wasn't even allowed to use.

Daphne kept trying to talk me into it.

> If we don't get enough help, I'll have to cancel. Or scale it back. Or just hope we get enough presents. We really need your help.

She sent a Star Wars GIF of Princess Leia saying, "Help me. You're my only hope." I snickered despite myself.

# WRAPPING PAPER RIVALS

> Let me think about it. I will help, but I don't know about being in charge of the entire thing.

> Totally get it. Though not sure who else I would ask.

> Pushing me isn't going to get me to agree. This time of year is insane.

> I know, I know. Sorry. I'm just tired and worried.

> I'm sure. Let me think on it. Send over whatever Jeffrey has done.

> Nothing electronic. It's literally on sticky notes and in a yellow legal pad. I didn't realize how disorganized he was.

I ground my teeth.

> Okay, I'll come to the meeting tomorrow at two. We can talk more then.

> You're the best.

She closed the conversation with the blowing kiss emoji, and I set my phone down, glancing at my computer. Eleven more online orders had come in.

What the hell was I going to do?

# CHAPTER 6

"I brought you some coffee!" Franklin, my assistant, exclaimed as he came in the back door from the alley. I sat in my little workstation in the storage room of my doll shop, surrounded by boxes, packing tape, and wrapping paper. There had been an additional eight online orders during the night, bringing the total up to forty-one different items needing to be wrapped, packaged, boxed, and made ready for shipping. And it was only the Saturday after Thanksgiving. We still had the entire month of December to deal with. It was overwhelming. I'd never had so many online orders placed in a single day. And I'd realized what had caused it; an article in the New York Times about unique toy shops on the East Coast had named me. I was grateful, but might need to hire more help at this rate. I'd already put in another order with my distributor, paying for the extra shipping to ensure I wasn't going to run out of toys this weekend.

"You are amazing." I curled my keyboard-stiffened fingers around the coffee cup and taking a sip. Black coffee with oat milk and a tiny pump of peppermint hit my tongue, raising my mood immediately.

"It's only eight a.m." Franklin looked around at the boxes sealed and ready for the post office and the number that still needed to be boxed. "What time did you get here? And how many orders do we have?"

Franklin had answered my help-wanted ad six months ago, and I'd never looked back. He was on the shorter and stockier side, with a friendly face, softened with wire-rim glasses and gentle blue eyes. I'd been hesitant to bring a male assistant into a doll store, but Franklin had a knack for charming the kids and their parents. He was especially skilled at calming child meltdowns when parents said no to a wanted item. It had been weeks since we'd had a tantrum in the store.

"I think I got here at six," I said. "Too many online orders to ignore."

"So I see." Franklin winced and looked at the pile of boxes. "If I knew you were going to come in so early to do this, I wouldn't have let you close last night."

"You had plans," I said and took a big sip of the coffee, the caffeine kicking in. I'd been up late and slept poorly. You'd think I'd be stressed about the dinner for the foster kids or how busy this Christmas season was going to be. But no, I'd been obsessing over Max, hoping he was okay, worried he'd freeze in the streets, and I'd never see him again. But of course, this morning I'd found the cat's bowl I'd left in the alleyway licked clean—which was a relief—but Max still hadn't come when I'd tried calling for him. "How were your plans?" I asked Franklin, trying to focus on the here and now.

He grimaced. "My friends invited someone they were trying to set me up with. She was very nice, but there was no connection. I mean, we had fun because we were with a big group, eating Thanksgiving leftovers, but I couldn't think of anything to say to her."

"And that's why I stopped dating," I said, saluting him with my cup.

He shrugged. "My friends won't let me quit yet. They're convinced they can find the right date for me. How'd things go here after I left?"

I groaned. "God, I had to reopen for this woman, who was very nice and who bought three of the Fashion Dream Doll accessories for a niece."

"That's not so bad. Least you didn't open for her to not buy anything." He started moving the packages, putting them into the big white carrying boxes I used for the post office.

"But here's the bad part. She's the sister of Patrick. That ... guy ... who runs that toy store over on Third. He lectured ME on how to run a toy store." And I told him all about my encounter with Patrick.

"I actually put on that podcast he recommended," I said as we ran tape over box seams, and printed out shipping labels. "I made it about eight minutes. It was all full of advice that I either knew ... like online orders." I eye rolled and looked at the boxes surrounding us. "Or conversations about how rich these guys were with their stock portfolios."

"I know those types of shows," Franklin said. "There's probably some good advice, but it's so general—"

"And not made for toy stores," I said. "And Patrick is right. Running a profitable toy store is hard, but if he thinks his way of doing it—just toys stacked on wire shelves—is the solution, then he's getting terrible advice. But after yesterday, I'm not going to be recommending his store anymore."

Franklin sighed. "That's tough. You two really don't compete. And if you don't send people to his store, then shoppers are going to go online in this area. And that may mean they stop coming here."

I pursed my lips. "I just don't think someone like him should be running a toy store. He doesn't like toys."

"And I agree." Franklin stood and stretched out his back. "But if you're not competing, it's just good karma. And takes a sale away from big box online stores."

Somehow, with Franklin's help, we finished all forty-seven orders within an hour. It was a Christmas miracle. I looked at the tidy boxes he'd stacked by the door. "Thank you for your help," I said. "Hell, I don't know what I'd do without you." I finished my coffee, saluting him with it. "And thank you for being my moral compass, too."

"Christmas bonus time is coming," he called over his shoulder as he went out into the store and began the opening process.

"Oh! I have to leave you in charge for a meeting," I told him. "About the foster kids' holiday dinner. Starts around two over at city hall. Apparently, nothing's been done, and Daphne is freaking out."

"No problem," he said and bent over to pick up the fuzzy brown teddy bear from where it had fallen last night. "Did Charles knock this over?" he asked, holding it up.

"Oh yeah," I said. "I'd forgotten about that. I told him goodnight, and he knocked over the teddy bear." Taking it from him, I picked my way up the iron staircase, making sure I didn't step on any of the other decorations.

"Jerk," Franklin muttered under his breath, then winced. "Hey!" he called out to the store. "Don't push me."

I snorted under my breath. I felt bad for the ghost—as much as his antics could be annoying—I couldn't imagine being trapped in one place, only able to communicate through cold spots, knocking stuff over, and messing with the electrical system. It must be a terrible way to spend your afterlife.

Franklin turned on the sound system and a pretty version of *Rocking Around the Christmas Tree* came on. I bobbed along with it as we made sure the store was ready for us to unlock the doors. It was five minutes to opening with several people waiting at the door when Mariah Carey came on again.

"Knock it off, Charles!" Franklin yelled. "No one likes this song." In response, the packages of doll clothes swung back and forth on their hangers in an invisible wind. I almost felt a chuckle breathed across my face.

"Come on, both of you," I said. "It's almost—"

Franklin's phone buzzed, and he pulled it out of his pocket. "Oh no," he exclaimed, going white.

"What's wrong?" I asked, my heart beginning to hammer.

"My parents were in a car accident!"

## CHAPTER 7

"What car accident? Are your parents okay?" I demanded.

"I don't know." His fingers moved furiously across his screen. "My sister thinks Dad might need surgery. They're getting transported to the hospital now."

"Oh no," I murmured. I wanted to ask more questions: how fast were they going? Which of them was the driver? Was the car totaled? Were other cars involved? Pedestrians? Passengers? But I knew Franklin didn't have any other information and would tell me when he could. He kept pausing to read his screen, then reply, fingers flying, lips moving as he typed out responses.

There was a knock on the front door, making the silver bell attached to the doorknob jingle. We were a minute past opening and customers were cupping their hands over their eyes, trying to see in through the window. I waved and raised a finger to show one minute.

They knocked again. Oh, this was going to be a fun group

of shoppers. I waved back, giving them the one-minute signal again and resisting the urge to use another finger.

"Why don't you go home?" I told Franklin, trying to be mindful of my customers. "For an hour or two; until you figure this out." He needed to focus, and being here wouldn't help.

He took off his glasses, wiping away a tear with shaking hands. "My sister is freaking out. She's ... she's ... not good at stuff like this. Depression, anxiety, all of that. I can't even get a good answer from her about what happened. But according to her, Mom is in the ER, and Dad is going into emergency surgery."

The door rattled as someone knocked hard on it. Oh, for God's sake! What was wrong with people?

"You're in no shape to work," I told him. "Go take a break in the back, at least. Call your sister and figure out what to do."

"I may have to fly to Denver, like tonight."

"Then you have to fly to Denver."

"But the store—"

"Will still be here," I said. "I've managed by myself at Christmas time. We'll be fine. Family first. Always. Just go sit in the back for a few minutes." I went to the front door, my hand ready to twist the lock open. "Just let me know how they're doing as soon as you know more."

"Thanks Kayla."

"Of course."

I took a deep breath, turning the lock, focusing on the moment, trying not to worry about Franklin's parents and what Christmas without Franklin might mean. I'd never met his parents, but knew he talked to them weekly. Hopefully, things weren't too serious, but his parents were elderly and accidents could—

I pushed the thoughts away.

"Sorry," I told the family waiting at the entrance when I swung the door open. "We had a bit of a crisis, but we're open now."

A blonde woman in a pink beanie took a deep breath, her lips tight, and her finger out to point at me, likely lecture me on the importance of time management, but her daughter's squeal of joy drowned it out. The finger went down, and the woman stepped into the store, looking around, her anger diffused, and wonder in her face. That was good because if she'd yelled at me, I'd likely have yelled back and thrown her out of my store. No sale was worth the drama from a drama-queen mom. Especially at Christmas time.

I felt a puff of air as Charles moved around me and knew I wasn't alone. The little girl and her mom disappeared down the Barbie aisle as more families shuffled in. Merchandise practically sparkled, the holiday lights twinkled, the Christmas music played, and I worked the cash register. The first few hours flew by, the silver bell on the front door at counterpoint to the chimes from the credit card machine. I smiled and wrapped, answered questions, put items into bags, and ran credit card after credit card as shoppers bought dollhouse furniture, doll clothing, and lots of dolls. Franklin stepped out from the back once, his face haggard, to tell me his dad was still in surgery, and he needed to leave immediately to catch his flight.

I paused, wrapping a Monster High doll to give him an enormous hug. "Keep me in the loop," I said.

"I'm sorry to leave like this," Franklin said, scrubbing his face like he was trying to scrub away the last few hours.

"Don't be. This will be fine." I so wanted to tell him that everything would be all right, his parents would be okay. I wanted to get lost in the platitudes but knew better. Life was a bitch sometimes. And if I told him everything would be fine, he'd know I was lying. Things wouldn't be fine; they'd just be different now.

I turned back to the customers, trying to create a perfect holiday for their child, focusing on the here and now. There was nothing else I could do for Franklin.

During a lull at one, I took a sip of my now cold coffee. I was starving, but this was the first moment I'd had without a line, and sure enough, a harried dad stepped up to the counter, setting five different Disney Princess dolls and two Bratz onto the counter. "Gift wrapping?" I asked.

"No thanks," he said, typing quickly on his phone. "Do you know of anywhere around here where I can get some less girly toys? Legos, or board games or something?"

"No sorry," I said. Franklin was a better person than I was. "Your best bet is going to be the shopping center in the next town over."

He glanced at the time and nodded tiredly. "I think I can make it there and back again. I need gifts for tonight; our online packages aren't going to arrive in time for the family party. You ever wished you could freeze time, or just add an extra hour on to a day?"

"All the time," I said and sighed. "Actually, I think there's a toy store down the road. They'll have what you want. I'd forgotten about them."

His eyes lit up, and I felt guilty for not saying something earlier. "Really? Just down the road?"

"Three blocks down." I gave directions, cringing that I was helping Patrick. But it wasn't fair for me to make this man's life harder because Patrick didn't know how to run a toy store.

"Thank you so much," he said, grabbing his bags and hurrying out to the street. My stomach gave a loud rumble.

I'd never be able to leave to grab lunch, let alone make the two o'clock meeting for the foster kids' dinner. I'd have to text Daphne and tell her I couldn't help with the dinner—not without Franklin to mind the store. Actually, I had no idea how I was going to run this store without him; not after that write up in the New York Times.

My stomach rumbled again, a wave of light-headedness hitting. Maybe there were stale granola bars in the back? Maybe I could text Taylor from the bakery across the street and ask him to bring me something? I grabbed my phone and started scrolling through my contacts, cursing myself for not saving his name like "Taylor from Decadent Treats" but had stupidly saved it by last name. And now I couldn't remember his last name.

A woman stepped up to the counter as I scrolled, and I was so tired all I could comprehend were her turquoise gloves. "Excuse me," she said. "Can I see your Madame Alexander Gone with the Wind doll?"

I blinked a few times. That doll was one of my more valuable ones, priced at $1485.00. Selling her would be a huge win, though I'd had that iconic doll wearing the green curtain dress complete with gold tassels since opening.

I'd miss her.

"Of course," I said, unlocking the case and shaking my head. Hunger was making me emotional. The woman examined the doll carefully, looking without touching; a true collector who knew grubby hands could damage the costume

"I have the box and everything, even the pink tissue paper," I said. "I can pull her out if you want to examine her more carefully."

The woman stepped back. "That's unnecessary, but I am going to think a bit more about it. That's quite a price tag, but I've been looking for one like her for years. Did you get her from an estate sale?"

I nodded. "The owner never displayed her, but kept her in acid-free tissue paper, keeping the pink folded underneath."

"Thank you," the woman said, pulling back on her gloves. "I'm in town for a few more days and I'll keep thinking about her." She took one last look while I locked up the case and left when I went back to the counter to ring someone up.

I looked at the doll—I'd have missed her, but that sale would have meant I could go all out for presents for Luke and his family. Oh well; maybe the woman would be back.

The front door jingled yet again as someone else stepped in. I sighed, but managed a cheery, "Hi there! Just let me know if you have any—" My words died. It was Lara, her cheeks pinked from the cold and a pale blue beret contrasting beautifully with her curly red hair.

"Hi!" she exclaimed with a wave, coming over to the checkout counter. "I just wanted to let you know my niece, Sage, loved the doll clothes you picked out. And the wrapping paper and just the whole present was amazing. She had an incredible birthday last night. And no, she did not spend the evening on her screen, but spent it playing with her doll."

"I'm so glad," I said, trying not to be weird. Lara had done nothing wrong. Her brother had been the asshole. Not her.

She licked her lips and looked down at the floor. "I also wanted to apologize," she said, her voice a little softer. "My brother—there's no excuse, but he's going through a lot. He's just ... I don't know ... I'm sure you picked up on the family drama. Long story short—very long story short—we don't get along with our step-siblings, though we do try. Kind-of. And I think Patrick's filter was low after working all day and then being around them. But he shouldn't have said what he did. I can tell how much you love toys." She looked around, stretching her head back to look at the chandelier casting its multi-colored light on everything. "Your store is beautiful, and you have the most interesting things. Is that a Victorian dollhouse?" she asked, pointing and then darting over. "Oh my gosh, you furnished the attic with little boxes, and trunks and portraits against the wall. That's the coolest thing! I wish I had a little girl so I could buy it 'for her,'" she said, using finger quotes.

"Thank you," I said. "That was a lot of fun to decorate. I also did one from the seventies and went all out on the crazy furnishings." I took Lara on a quick tour of the dollhouses I had on display; the 70s townhome, the modern one with glass and iron furniture, and the cabin I'd furnished like it was on a lake, complete with wood paneling.

"These are so cool! They're like art!"

"Thank you. They're fun hobbies and the cool thing is that I get to make money off my hobby."

"I can see that," Lara said. "But what I'm really here to do is to apologize for my brother and give you an apology snack." She reached into her purse and pulled out a bag from Decadent Treats.

Normally I'd have refused, but my stomach gave another rumble. I peeked inside the bag to see a frosted sugar cookie glistening with crystallized red and green sugar and three of my favorite cookies—snickerdoodles.

"You didn't have to. I'd practically forgotten about the whole thing," I lied. I'd just wanted to put the whole thing out of my mind.

"Well, it's Christmas time. Also, I brought in the toys for the foster kids from the ornaments I collected last night." She held up a plain brown bag. "I confess, I did buy them from my brother's store, but I used his discount. And I didn't think the kids would care."

"No, they don't," I said. "And I think your brother donates some toys to the foster kids as well."

"See, so he's not a monster," Lara said.

I put the toys behind the counter. "Never thought he was." I reached into the bakery bag and folded a bite of the sugar cookie into my mouth, instantly feeling better. Nothing like sugar on an empty stomach.

"Well, Patrick can be a monster," she said. "This one time, he cut the hair off my Barbies. I've only just now forgiven him."

I laughed. "Is he older or younger than you?"

"Older," Lara said glumly. "About five years. He got to move out when ... all the family drama happened."

I had to admit; I was dying to find out more. Why did they hate their step-siblings and why had they even come into town for Thanksgiving?

My phone buzzed, Daphne's name popping up on the screen. "Excuse me," I told Lara before I could get into the gossip.

"Oh, of course," she responded. "I'm going to do some shopping. I have a hankering to learn more about dollhouses." She headed down one of the aisles and I smiled. Who used the word hankering anymore?

"Hey Daphne. I'm glad you called. I'm—"

"Please, please, please tell me you're going to make it to the meeting," she interrupted. "No one else is available, or they have COVID, or are leaving town or some other made-up excuse, and if we can't get this going, I'm going to have to cancel the entire holiday dinner. And you know this is the only holiday treat some of these kids get."

My heart sank. "Oh no," I said. "But here's the thing—"

"No, don't you dare," she hissed. "I don't have anyone else. You don't have to be in charge, but you do need to help."

"Look," I said, picking at a small glob of coffee on the counter. "I can't come to the meeting at two. Franklin's parents just got into a horrible car accident and he's catching a plane to Denver. I don't have anyone to mind the store. I don't even know—"

"I can cover the store." Lara came back up to the counter clutching books about dolls and dollhouses. "I was eavesdropping; I'm sorry. But if you have to go to a meeting at two, I can cover. With some quick lessons on how to ring people up, of course. But I've done sales before. And long as I tell people I'm just covering, they'll understand and know I can't answer all their questions. I can take down names and numbers if I need to. And it's just an hour or two, right?"

Mariah Carey came onto the store's speakers and the silver bell on the front door rang loudly, though no one had touched the door—Charles' way of either agreeing or cautioning me. I wished the ghost could talk plain English rather than communicating through bell ringing and freaking Mariah Carey.

"Let whoever that is mind the store," Daphne ordered. "I really need the help."

"But—"

"I can totally do it," Lara said. "It would be fun. And I have nothing else to do today."

Oh hell. Would Daphne really cancel the foster kids' dinner if I didn't come to the meeting?

# CHAPTER 8

*I* massaged my temple, willing away the headache I was getting, while Daphne continued to push. "If we don't get some of the local businesses to help, we won't be able to do the dinner. Truly. I can't pull this off without help, and no one can help. These kids, of all kids, deserve to have a happy Christmas. You know that!"

I'd never told Daphne I'd been a foster kid. I was unique among many foster kids because I hadn't been taken away from my mom by social workers or a well-meaning judge. My mom just couldn't take care of me in that moment—I'd done therapy and worked my way through the multitude and complex emotions I had toward my mom. I now realized she'd done the best she could, as a single mom who didn't get any money from my dad, an unknown entity in my life. And up until I was six, we'd been coping fine. She'd found money to pay the bills; we had enough food and a bit of extra money for the occasional luxury. But then mom was laid off from her receptionist job and there were a few weeks where she didn't go to work at all. When she'd found another job, it had paid less and was further away. Then the car got a flat tire, and I got a sinus infection, and she had to call out of work. They'd fired her and she'd sold a few things to get the money together to pay for the tire and antibiotics. The next day my mom had broken a tooth and needed it pulled, which she didn't have the money for.

I remembered my last dinner with her had consisted of two stale crackers, a tiny portion of forgotten pasta collected off the pantry shelf, and a cup of warmed water I'd pretended was tea. She didn't eat at all, though I tried to share; she probably hadn't eaten all day.

The next day and the day after that, there was no food. I remembered whining about being hungry and my mom bursting into tears, hugging me close. The next morning, she got me up, put my clothes and toys in a suitcase, and drove me to some bored woman's office where I sat in an uncomfortable chair clutching the suitcase while my mom filled out paperwork, her tears leaking onto the page.

I'd never seen her again, though I had gotten cards and emails from her for the first few years. They'd stopped when I was eleven. When I became pregnant with Luke, I tried to find her, but she'd completely disappeared. At the time, and with the narcissistic lens of a teenager, I thought she'd changed her name to get away from me. But I now knew she'd never have stopped checking on me if it was in her control. She'd probably died, though I doubted I'd ever find out for sure.

Christmases as a foster kid were the worst, when you were lucky to be remembered, to get a gift, any gift, even if it was socks and a warm hat. Though I wasn't being fair—there were good families out there, doing the best they could, but it always seemed like there were more foster kids who knew there was no Santa and didn't expect him to show up.

"Please Kayla," Daphne said into my phone. "I don't want to cancel this dinner. I know you don't want that either."

I remembered knowing there were no gifts under the tree for me. I remembered that sick feeling of resignation laced with despair that foster kids like me tried to push down so no one could use it against us. I wasn't Santa, but maybe Lara showing up in the nick of time was the closest I'd get to a Christmas miracle. And I couldn't give Christmas miracles, but I could at least go to the meeting if nothing else.

"Okay, I'll be there," I told Daphne and disconnected the call before she could ask for anything else. I turned to Lara. "Let's give you a crash course on how to run this place."

Lara was a quick learner, picking up how to ring up purchases within a few tries. "If anyone needs anything you can't answer, just tell them I'll be back by three thirty, at the latest."

"Not a problem," Lara said. "Most people are pretty understanding. And those that aren't—you don't want their business, anyway."

I touched her arm. "Thank you."

"Of course." She grinned, her green eyes dancing. "This is going to be the highlight of my day. I'm working in a doll store!" She gave a little shimmy. "I mean, looking at all the dollhouses and Barbies are bringing back all sorts of memories. I had so much fun with my dolls as a little girl."

"A lot of little girls did," I said. "You have my cell; call if you need anything."

"I will. But it will be fine." She shooed me out.

Buttoning my coat and putting on my beanie and gloves, I dashed out the back door and trotted the six blocks to city hall. The temperature was definitely dropping, a light dusting of snow covering the traditional city Christmas decorations, making the city look like a holiday card. In the evening, the lights would turn it magical, a perfect Christmas memory. It was no wonder people drove over thirty miles to do their Christmas shopping in our little town.

I climbed the steps into City Hall and walked through the double doors, heading to Daphne's office, the utilitarian space livened by pictures of her kids. "We're meeting in the conference room," she said, gathering a laptop, a stack of various sizes and colors of used sticky notes, and an iPad. "I've got all the notes from Jeffrey's office, and that's it. I've had no time to prep, and no time to put together a project management spreadsheet. We'll just wing this meeting. Not that it matters, since I think you're the only one who confirmed they were coming."

"Let me take some of that," I said, taking the laptop into my arms and walking with her down the hallway. I could tell Daphne was stressed, her pale skin blotchy with anxiety. Her hands holding the papers trembled.

"You okay?" I asked. "You're shaking."

"Just too much caffeine. Too much to do. I really hope more business owners show up today and I can assign some of these tasks. My team can't do it all. I'm so disappointed in Jeffrey. I thought he was further along, or you know ... had done anything."

We walked into the empty conference room, and I looked at my watch. 2:03. This wasn't good. I glanced at Daphne—there were actual tears in her eyes. But she breathed deep and pulled out a chair at the giant oval table. This conference room was in heavy use—you could tell from the faint smell of coffee, crumbs of breakfast sandwiches, the dings on the walls from the chairs and the glass boards that still held dry erase marker echoes from previous meetings. The chairs were all askew, none pushed in to the table.

"God, this place is a mess," Daphne said, swiping the

crumbs from the table. "Well, it's just you and me. Let's start by going through the checklist. The biggest thing we need is a caterer." She handed me a list of local restaurants. "Do you think you can call these sometime today? It should be for about 150 people, ideally under $10 a person. I don't want to do pizza and burgers—"

"No," I interrupted. "It should be fancier than that."

"Agreed. So try to stay in budget. But if it's higher, let me know. We don't want super cheap food, like last year. Lean on the fact that it's for foster kids and maybe they'll donate or reduce the fee. I think Jeffrey's managed to pull that off in prior years."

"Do you know who you used last year? Maybe we can ask them. Though the food last year was terrible!"

Daphne made a face. "The Tasty Fork."

"Didn't they close a few months ago for like cockroaches and health code violations?"

"Yep," Daphne said.

"I ate that last year," I said, my stomach swimming, the cookies I'd had for lunch threatening to come back up.

"We all did," Daphne said, pulling a sticky note off a pile, squinting and typing on her computer.

"We fed that to foster kids! That's a walking cliché! Government can't afford a good caterer, so give the foster kids the food from the one with a rat-infested kitchen. Hell no."

Daphne raised an eyebrow and leaned back in her chair. "First, there weren't rats that I know of. Second, we didn't know. And third, yes, maybe Jeffrey went too cheap with the catering budget. I can talk to him once he's back. But for now, that's not a problem I can fix. You're right, it is clichéd, though. God, what a mess this is." She breathed deep, blinking back tears.

Guilt lurched in my chest. I was being too mean. Daphne had come into work the Saturday after Thanksgiving to figure this out. I looked around the empty room. It was just me and Daphne. Maybe I could ask Lara for help—she seemed like the type who'd want to get involved, though I knew nothing about the other woman. Did she work? Have a family? How much free time did she have?

"I'll get it done," I said.

Daphne wiped away a tear and, trying for humor, waggled her eyebrows. "I take it you'll find a non-rat-infested caterer."

I laughed. "I'll do my best."

"Thank you. On to the next thing—organizing the—"

The door to the conference room opened and Patrick walked in. "Sorry, I'm late," he said. "It was hard to get away from the—" He spotted me. "Oh good, you got away too. I mean, sorry." He pushed his glasses up his nose. "I mean, you get it. It's Christmas time and everyone seems to need something and it's hard to get away from the store. But I made it." He pulled out a chair and sat down.

"What are you doing here?" I asked. Why would someone like him care about helping the foster kids' dinner?

"Helping," he said with a frown. "Daphne said we all needed to pitch in."

"We got this," I said.

"Who is this we?" Daphne asked, looking around the empty conference room. "Right now, it's just the two of us. We need help."

But I didn't want help from him! He raised an eyebrow at me. "You okay? You want me to get you some coffee?"

Damn it. He was being nice. And I couldn't help but notice he wasn't wearing a flannel like every other guy in Penduline Village. Instead, his emerald button-up matched his eyes, the same eyes his sister had. There was just enough scruff on his chin to make you think of breakfasts in bed and his shoulders seemed to fill the room. He must spend hours at the gym. Again, the image of the moms flooding his store, holding dollar bills up to ... woah. Now I was comparing him to an erotic dancer. Hell, what was wrong with me? I shook away the image. "Sorry," I muttered. "I skipped lunch and was at the store super early for the online orders."

"What can I do?" Patrick asked.

"We're trying to put together a list, based on these," Daphne waved around Jeffrey's pile of sticky notes. "And Kayla's in charge of the caterer. You want to organize presents or decorations?"

"Ummmm ... I was thinking more of RSVPs? Something easy," Patrick said.

"That is the one thing I can put the interns in charge of," Daphne said. "And I have the list of families who said they were interested in coming. We'll have to do confirmations, but that can wait until we're closer." She tugged on a lip, thinking. "Okay, what do we have to have?"

"Food and presents," I supplied. "A Santa. And a Christmas tree."

"I can do a Christmas tree," Patrick said. "I actually—"

"Christmas trees and decorations are pretty easy," Daphne interrupted. She was flipping through Jeffrey's sticky notes, trying to organize them, though several had gotten folded or stuck to each other. "There's a bunch of trees and decorations still in storage, I think. Oh, here we go," she said, separating a sticky note and waving it around. "We need dessert."

"Dessert?" Patrick asked.

"Oh yeah," I said. "That picture." Last year, a volunteer had taken a beautiful picture of several of the kids, their hands full of cookies and colored crumbs on their lips while the Christmas lights shone in the background. The City Hall had used that picture in their requests for funding for the foster kids' program and for activities for them. And more importantly, the kids had loved the treats.

"Yep, I almost forgot," Daphne said. "You need to call all the local bakeries and try to get them to donate cookies or a cake or pies or something," she said. "We can't afford to pay for the desserts, but the desserts are a key part of the dinner. Did you come last year?"

Patrick shook his head, but I knew what she was talking about. The dessert table had been immensely popular last year.

"I think cookies are key. We might get a volunteer to bake some if nothing else. Oh, I have an idea," I said, snapping my fingers. "Let's do a cookie decorating station. I felt like last year, some kids, especially the teenagers, were bored."

Patrick frowned. "That's going to be super—"

Daphne pointed a finger gun at me. "Yes! Actually, a cookie decorating station might be really fun. We just get cheap cookies and lots of decorations. Super easy to get donated." She typed on her laptop, the keys clicking. "So let's focus on getting the bakeries to donate pies or cakes," she said to Patrick, "While we get the volunteers to make cookies."

"Are we really promoting sugary treats to these kids?" Patrick asked. "Doesn't that send the wrong message? Diabetes? Too much sugar? Poor eating? And isn't feeding foster kids sugar a bit of a cliché?"

"It's Christmas time," I said, rolling my eyes. "I think it's the one time of year we can't do too much to spoil these kids."

"But of all kids, don't they need to learn good nutrition? I mean, how many of these 'parents,'" he actually did air quotes, "just throw sugar at them to get them to be quiet and go away?"

Okay, he had a point. But not one I was going to let him win.

"But it's Christmas time," I said. "Some of these kids are lucky if they get McDonalds thrown their way. That's a treat for many of them."

"See, that's my point," Patrick said. "I mean, poor nutrition can follow foster kids, because so many don't take the time to teach them good nutrition. There's a great podcast I was—"

Hell no, not podcasts again.

"But. It's. Christmas. Time!" I said again. "If their poor nutritional education bothers you so much, go volunteer to teach classes to the foster homes. Go to their homes and pass out fruit and veggie baskets. But these kids—"

"Patrick raises a good point," Daphne said. "We do need to offer some fruit, some sugar-free candy, and that type of thing. We should make sure we're being inclusive to any kids with diabetes or who are on a special diet. Isn't there gluten in cookies?"

"But they can't decorate fruit," I said, hunger and irritation making my voice sharp.

"Okay." Daphne sighed deeply. "God, this is taking so much longer than it should." She typed frantically on her laptop. "It's a good thing I like you and the decorating station is a great idea. We'll offer paper cookies with markers for those that don't or can't have the sugar." She scribbled and let out another sigh. "And God help me, we'll offer glittery glue, so it's like icing, so there's no drama."

"Thank you," Patrick said stiffly.

I pushed down my annoyance. He was right—statistically,

foster kids ate poorly for a multitude of reasons, but Christmas wasn't like the rest of the year. For one evening, it shouldn't matter. The foster kids' dinner was about giving a good evening to kids who may not have many good evenings. It did seem like he cared about the kids, I grumbled to myself. Why couldn't I just dislike him? Why did he have to do nice things like care about foster kids' nutrition?

"Okay, so food, we've got a plan for," Daphne typed, presumably adding to her project management spreadsheet. "Let's head over to decorations. We've got fake trees in storage we can put up. Can you both come in early on the 21st to help decorate?"

"Four days before Christmas?" Patrick and I said together. "Not unless Franklin is back," I said. "And even then, it takes two people to mind the store in the days before Christmas. That's my busiest time of the year."

"Who's watching your store now?" Patrick asked.

"Your sister," I snapped.

Embarrassment churned in my stomach. Oh God, I'd made it sound like some joke from the 90s.

His head slowly turned toward me. "Are you kidding?"

Ummm... "No. And I know that sounded terrible, but she volunteered. I'm not being a smart-ass."

"Wait, she's really watching your store? Lara? Why is she there? How is she there?"

They were fair questions, but who was he to interrogate me? Yep, I was back to disliking him. "'Cause she offered to help when I needed help. Or I wouldn't—"

"And we're grateful she did," Daphne said, cutting through the brewing storm. "So that's a no-go on you being able to help decorate," she muttered. "I'll guilt someone else into helping."

"I can probably help," Patrick said. "I have more than one

# WRAPPING PAPER RIVALS

employee. I don't think I could run a successful business without more than just one person to help." He touched my hand. "I can help you find someone. I just use college kids. One is a lot like another. Pay them minimum wage, make sure they don't work enough to need benefits or anything. They call out, and spend too much time on their phones, but they're fast on the cash register and that's all anyone cares about; getting in and out and saving time."

There was so much wrong with his statement that my mouth fell open. First, I didn't need his help to find a random college student to "assist" me. Second, I was not looking for someone to work the cash register as fast as they could. Third, I definitely didn't want staff who called out and spent too much time on their phone, ignoring the customers. And fourth, I took care of my people. Christmas was rough, but that was okay because it helped to pay for the rest of the year, including paying Franklin fairly for his time. My toy store wasn't a squeeze-as-much-money-out-of-the-town as possible business. It was my dream and a way I could make people's lives a bit better.

I tried not to see red. "Mr. Toys Are Disposable" was apparently "Mr. People Are Disposable" too. I couldn't imagine walking into a toy store as a parent and seeing the person at the cash register scrolling through social media on their phone, not caring about the shopping experience.

I stared at Patrick. Somehow, we both owned toy stores on two different planets. How was that even possible?

"I think I'll have my interns organize who gets which present," Daphne continued to mutter to herself, typing, a pen gripped between her teeth. "And then we'll just need to organize a gift-wrapping party, but we'll figure that out once it's closer." The alarm on her phone went off, and I startled. "Okay, that's my signal to get home. It's a Saturday, and I got things to do. Good job," she said, not picking up on how annoyed I was with Patrick. "But please bug the other business owners into helping and please get back to me ASAP with the caterer and the desserts." She collected her laptop and paperwork and ran out the door, leaving me alone with Patrick. I gave him a tight-lipped smile and grabbed my purse and jacket.

"Looks like we're going to be working together more," he said.

"I guess so." Nothing I wanted less in this entire world. Maybe we needed to create territories along Main Street. He could have the west side; I could have the east. I wanted to laugh and cry at the same time. God, I was so hungry and tired.

He stood up, and began to organize the conference room chairs, absently, like their disorganization bugged him. "But I have a question."

Oh hell, now what?

"Why is my sister watching your store?"

# CHAPTER 9

I pushed past Patrick, easily able to move through the conference room now that he'd tidied up the chairs. I needed to get back to my store. "Look," I told Patrick. "You'd have to ask your sister that question. I'm not in charge of her. She volunteered. I'm not taking advantage."

I looped my purse over my shoulder, pulling on my gloves and beanie hat as I walked down the utilitarian hallway past the formal and corporate pictures of my city council members. "I don't see why it matters though, even if you're her big brother. Do you feel like you have to give her permission or something?"

He snorted and fell into step with me. "I mean, she's always done what she wanted. History degree. Biochemistry degree. Med school. RN school. Teaching degree. I'm just surprised you would let a stranger manage your store without you there."

"Why shouldn't I?" Though he was right, I knew that.

"She's not going to do anything, but she could. You don't know her."

He was raising some good concerns, but I wasn't going to tell him that. And judging from the turnout of this meeting—a whole three people—I was needed to help figure out this dinner. Though I had no idea how I'd find the time to even go to the meetings, let alone call caterers. Maybe I could just send out a blanket email, or put the request onto a business Facebook or Linked-In group? That would totally work, right?

And why had I let Lara run my store? It wasn't like me. "I happen to be a very trusting person," I lied. "You don't know me."

"True," he said. "But judging from your store, I would've said you were a bit of a perfectionist."

I felt my cheeks redden. There was nothing wrong with perfectionism. It had gotten me a doll store routinely mentioned in travel blog posts and had over 500 Yelp reviews. I had 4.6 stars, and a write up in the New York Times, thank you very much, jerk-wad.

I should check how many stars he had. I bet he had five reviews total, 2.6 stars, and they all said his store sucked.

"I own a doll store," I snapped. "I'm not selling purses or jewelry. Your sister's not going to run off with a dollhouse and sell it to tourists out of her trunk." Even if she stole one of the valuable dolls, it wasn't like someone would buy it for 50% off. They were niche for very niche collectors.

He chuckled under his breath. Was he enjoying this argument? God, he was weird. Good looking, but weird. "I'm just surprised she went in there again. I mean, it hasn't even been twenty-four hours, and while your store is charming, it's not really her scene."

This should be fun. "She came to apologize," I said. "For your behavior yesterday."

"My behavior?" He frowned. "Wait. What did I do? I

## WRAPPING PAPER RIVALS

mean, I know I was in a hurry last night, but I don't remember saying—"

"How you said toys were disposable? That they're not important? That my store, the dolls I sell that hundreds of children have come to love, indoctrinate girls into traditional female roles? You even referenced a podcast I needed to listen to."

"Well, that's not quite—" The front doors of the building swished open and the cold hit me, taking my breath away. Clouds had gathered in the east, dark against the sky, and the temperature was dropping fast. We were in for a snowstorm, though my weather app hadn't warned me about it. I'd have to find Max, or he may not survive the night. But first I had to get back to my store.

"N'Easter's blowing in," Patrick said, stuffing his hands into his jeans' pockets. "I gotta get the house ready. Do you mind giving me my sister back? We've been cleaning it out and there's a lot of stuff I need to move."

Before I could say anything, a chilly wind shot straight through my coat, making my teeth chatter. I buttoned it up before pulling on my gloves. Next to me, Patrick shivered, trying to stuff his bare hands further into his pockets. "Where's your jacket?" I asked. And then wondered why I was mothering him. It wasn't any of my business.

He looked around like he expected it to magically appear on the ground at his feet. "Probably back at my store." He shifted from foot to foot, the icy wind ruffling his blonde hair, and pinking his cheeks. "I think I got off on the wrong foot with you. I can tell we're on different sides of the toy debate. But I think I made you mad. And I didn't mean to."

Mad? Different sides? That was like one side thinking shrimp were like bugs, and shouldn't be consumed, while the other thought shrimp was the best delicacy ever. He thought toys were disposable, that they didn't matter! My guilt disappeared. That wasn't different sides. How could there be two sides to thinking toys were valuable or not? He'd obviously never seen a scared four-year-old holding a stuffed animal like it was the only thing keeping her safe in the universe. He'd never cried himself to sleep when some foster "parent" had thrown away the doll he'd received under a Christmas tree because he'd forgotten to unload the dishwasher.

The memories punched through me, and I had to take a deep breath, so they didn't drag me into a panic attack. My knees began to tremble with emotion and cold.

"But I want this holiday dinner for the foster kids to go off well," Patrick continued, not realizing I was pushing back anxiety. "Foster kids need a good holiday event to look forward to. And they do like getting presents. And I'd like to work with you. I think two toy store owners are the perfect hosts for something like this."

"Even if the toys they're getting are disposable?" I said, my teeth beginning to chatter. I needed to get back to my store, relieve Lara, and get warm.

"How many kids have rooms full of toys they never play with?" he said. "I mean, it's kept me in business, don't get me wrong. And don't pretend you don't make a profit because the little girls and their parents are always buying new doll clothes and accessories. How many of those doll clothes aren't just left in a box somewhere, played with once or twice?"

He was right; I knew it, but he was so wrong, too. How many of those girls grew into teenagers or adults who looked on those toys with affection, remembering the joy they had dressing up their dolls and playing with them? How many of those girls passed their dolls and clothes onto their daughters and even granddaughters?

"Don't you ever watch the kids playing with toys? See them using their imagination, working through social niceties, working through their fears and emotions?" I asked.

He shrugged. "Not really. Seems creepy and weird to watch kids."

"You own a toy store! Don't you watch how they play so you know what to order? What to display? Doesn't one of your pod—"

A gust of chilly wind blew straight through my layers, and he let out a shiver. "Tell you what—we're both going to freeze out here. How about I take you out to coffee tonight and you can keep convincing me toys are valuable? I mean, we can work on the foster holiday dinner too, if you want," he continued. "I'm sure there's plenty more to do than get a caterer, get cakes and build a cookie decorating station." He grinned, his eyes lighting up his face. He really was handsome with his blonde hair and green eyes, the cold making his cheeks pink. And I was a sucker for tall men.

"The bakery across the street from your store makes an amazing Americana," he continued, giving me a side-grin.

Wait, was he asking me on a date? We barely knew each other and had argued each time. How was I date material? He probably had women lining up to—nope, not going there again. God, maybe it was time to consider dating again. But not him. We were too different in too many ways.

"I have plans tonight," I lied. "Sorry." Though I didn't know what I was apologizing for. He was the one asking me out.

He hunched his shoulders and took his hands out of his pockets to blow on them, rocking from foot to foot to keep warm. "No problem," he said. "Maybe tomorrow. Can you tell my sister to come by my store when she's done with yours? I want to talk to her."

Why was he using me as his messenger? Why didn't he just text her?

But before I could say anything, he gave me a small wave and jaywalked across the street toward his store. I turned in the opposite direction, trotting as quick as I could to get my blood flowing and get warm.

That had been weird. Right?

# CHAPTER 10

I unlocked the back door to my store but paused before turning the doorhandle. There was a strange sound coming from inside. Was that ... I opened the door, hearing Mariah Carey on so loud it practically knocked me back a step. I groaned; I'd forgotten to tell Lara about Charles. Though I had no idea how to bring up a ghost in casual conversation. *'So, you see, random stranger who's helping me—my store is also haunted.'* Yeah, that would've gone over well. Franklin had figured it out after a few weeks and had come to me, shaking, to let me know he thought the store was haunted. He'd almost quit.

I made a mental note to text Franklin and see how his parents were doing.

I stepped inside, wanting to put my hands over my ears. Charles had taken advantage of Lara to do what he wanted. Which was playing Mariah Carey on full blast. I rolled my eyes, draping my coat across the office chair in the back, and pulling off my gloves and beanie, slipping through the door and into the shop, the holiday lights, and sight of all the dolls, accessories, and dollhouses lifting my mood.

Lara waved from the counter. "You're back!" she exclaimed. "I was about to text you. I don't know what to do. Mariah Carey is on repeat, on super loud, and I can't figure out how to turn it off. And I just can't listen to this song anymore. Oh, here it comes," she said. The grand, "YOUUU-UUUUUUUUU," she sang along with the music. "Make it stop, Kayla. Make it stop!" She was smiling, but there was an edge of insanity that hadn't been there before.

"I got it," I said and unplugged the speaker. The music stopped, letting me hear the shuffle of cloth, the patter of boots, and the murmurs of customers talking about the merchandise or their lives. I plugged back in the device and asked it to play some instrumental Christmas music, turning down the sound.

"I tried that," Lara said. "Mariah just kept coming back. I probably should've left it unplugged."

"Yeah … ummm … there's a …" I couldn't tell her. Not with people in the store. "The wires here are weird. Old building. It's like it has a mind of its own sometimes."

The silver bell on the front door chimed, though no one was near it. The teddy bear swan dived off the balcony. Luckily, none of the customers were close to it, though I heard one say, "did you see that?"

Was Charles expressing his irritation at me turning off Mariah Carey? Or maybe irritated I wasn't telling Lara about him? Or was he just in a cranky mood with all the holiday drama?

"That was weird," Lara said, walking over and picking up the bear.

"Old building," I said again. "I probably didn't put it up

there securely. Maybe the heat clicked on or a truck drove by outside."

Lara patted the teddy bear and placed it behind the counter. "Or you have a ghost. All old buildings do." But before I could say anything, a nine or ten-year-old came up, clutching her purse and putting a Monster High doll on the counter. The child's mother hovered in the background, ready to step in, if necessary.

Lara picked up the doll box. "This one's fun," she said. "She's a little vampire. I like her pink striped hair."

"It's for my sister," the little girl said. "She already has Frankiestein. But Draculaura is her favorite. Her new favorite. She changes her favorite all the time."

"As wise women do. Are you getting it for her for Christmas?" Lara rang up the purchase, wrapping, and bagging with expertise.

"Yep." The little girl carefully pulled two twenties from her purse and passed them over. Lara counted out the change onto the counter, the girl's lips moving as she silently counted with Lara, before scooping the cash back into the purse.

"I know she'll love it," Lara said. She waved at the mom as the two customers left.

I needed to hire Lara. She was amazing with children. I mentally reviewed my budget. Could I make that happen? I still had Franklin on the books, but if he wasn't working, I wasn't paying him. But would that hurt his feelings to know I'd found a replacement so quickly? And would she even be interested? And what would I do with Franklin? Surely Lara would want to go back to her life, but what was that? Maybe I should take her out for drinks after work and get the scoop on her life.

*And Patrick's life,* a little voice whispered in my head. Wait—where'd that come from? I didn't care about him.

"How did things go here? Any problems?" I asked, straightening up a few things behind the counter as more customers continued to come in, the silver bell on the door jingling non-stop. Today might be my top day ever, beating yesterday, if I took online sales into account.

"No problems," she said. "I did have someone come in interested in one of the 20-inch Madame Alexander dolls you had in the case. The one in the green dress."

"Did she have turquoise gloves?" I couldn't believe that the woman had come back, and I'd missed her.

"Yep. She was asking me all these questions, like if you had the box," Lara continued, tugging on her lip. "And if the box had shelf damage, and if the doll had been displayed before or in a smoking home, and I couldn't answer those."

I raised an eyebrow. "Rats. I didn't think she'd come back so quickly. Did she seem like she was ready to buy?"

Lara shrugged. "I didn't get that feeling; more that she just wanted to take another look. But she said she'd be back tomorrow, and I took down her name and number too, just in case." She handed me a slip of paper.

"You're awesome." I stepped aside so Lara could ring up a little girl and her father buying a Barbie and a set of doll clothes. Lara again chatted with the family, finding out the Barbie was a Christmas present for a younger cousin. I watched the little girl's eyes light up when Lara approved of the purchase and proclaimed the little girl was a great cousin.

I just loved the light on a child's face when they bought a gift they knew someone else would love. This was one of the many reasons I owned a toy store. Why hadn't Patrick ever seen that? Had he just never looked for it, or just never experienced it? Or had he forgotten what it was like to be a child?

"But everything else went well," Lara said, interrupting my thoughts about her brother, which, let's be honest, was a good thing. "Did you figure out the foster kids' dinner?"

"Not yet," I said. "It's a bit of a mess; nothing's been done. So I got assigned finding a caterer and have a giant list of people to call. Then I have to hope they stay within budget."

"I can do those phone calls," Lara said. "Or I can mind the store, so you can do it."

"Oh no, you've done enough." Why was she being so helpful? I'd only met her yesterday, and this woman had given up her afternoon to mind my store, and now was offering to do even more?

Lara rang up another purchase, a baby doll this time, chatting with the older shopper—an elegant woman with a swoop of graying hair and a blue pashmina—discovering the woman had several grandkids, mostly boys. She'd been so excited to shop for dolls in my store rather than Patrick's.

"I like yours better," the woman confessed, looking at my multi-colored chandelier, the murals of trees and mythical creatures on the walls and the glittery floor. "It's elegant and whimsical and feminine without being all pink and white," she said. "That other store is just toys stacked on shelves and tables."

I nodded, feeling an odd combination of happiness and guilt. It was also awkward getting the comments in front of Lara—I really shouldn't be bashing her brother; not with all the help she'd given me today.

But Lara wasn't shy. "I've been telling my brother for months that he needs to do something more with that toy store. Something more like this. But he says it's not necessary. That the toys will sell regardless of what the toy store looks like."

"Your brother owns Toys and Games over on Third?" the woman stuttered, her cheeks blotching with red.

"He does, but I completely agree with you," Lara said with a wink. "I don't control him or approve of his store. Not after seeing this one." The woman smiled awkwardly, collecting her purchases and leaving, the damn bell echoing through the store when the door closed.

I went over and took the bell off. There was no need for it; not with the store being so busy. Maybe I'd put it back in January.

"Can I ask…" I turned to Lara. "Why are you helping me? You have to admit, it's a bit odd."

Lara raised an eyebrow. "Odder than you giving me control of your store while you left?"

"Okay, fair," I muttered, stuffing the silver bell under the counter. I'd put it away in the back later.

"Because you needed the help, and I was in the right place and right time," Lara said.

"I mean, how do you have the time?" I asked, stumbling a bit. "It's a Saturday, on Thanksgiving weekend and most people—" God, this conversation was going nowhere. My cheeks warmed. "I mean, I appreciate the help," I clarified. "I just ... you must still have family in town. And we met last night and now you're helping me run my store when your brother owns another toy store a few blocks away."

"My step-family left this morning. But are you really asking why I'm not helping him? Or are you asking why I don't have a job?"

"The brother part," I said. "Not the job part, though I suppose the brother part really isn't my business either."

Lara tugged on her lip. "I like your store better," she said.

"His store is kind-of depressing. And as for why I have the time..." she took a deep breath. "I got divorced a few months ago and haven't really found my footing. There's not a lot of jobs around here, it's a tourist town, so I'd be looking at a commute and blech." She stuck her tongue out. "And Patrick's and my grandfather just died and there's been things that need to be done. And if we're being nosy, Patrick is struggling right now. He moved in to help with Gramps a few years ago, and he was pretty attached to him. He's a bit lost after Gramps' death."

"I'm so sorry," I said, though I didn't know if I was apologizing for the divorce, the death of her grandfather, or for the feeling of being so lost.

"Thank you," Lara said. "It's okay—he went quickly, which is good. In terms of the divorce, it was both of our faults, I'm in therapy, and will figure out my path. But I'm not in a hurry."

"I'm so sorry," I said again. "I shouldn't have pried."

"It's a fair question. This random woman appears, is the sister of your competition, and is offering to help, and you don't know me. I get it. So to answer your question, I'm in town because Patrick needed help going through Gramp's house and I'm a little unrooted now. That's the simple story." She pulled her phone from a pocket and looked at the time. "I should probably get going, anyway."

"Thank you for your help." My words felt inadequate. Maybe I should offer to pay her or something.

"I had fun," she said, and darted into the back room to grab her purse and jacket. "Patrick did a good job of helping Gramps keep the house tidy, but there's all these rooms, and the attic and basement are completely full of random stuff. I'm happy to take breaks. I don't like being cooped up in it."

"Totally understand," I said. "By the way, Patrick says to come and see him once you're done here."

"Oh, he was at that meeting for the foster kids' dinner? Good for him. Though he could've just texted me," she said with an eye roll.

I chuckled. "That's what I said. Why am I his personal assistant?"

"He's just kind-of like that." She shrugged. "Just says whatever he's thinking. He's not mean, but it comes off a bit absentminded. Well, I'll go see what he needs. Do you want me to come back tomorrow and break you for lunch, since you don't have an assistant?"

That would be amazing! "No thank you," I demurred. "I don't want to take advantage."

"Oh, you're not," Lara said, her eyes going wide. "I just told you, Kayla; I needed a break from that damn house."

I laughed. "Okay, then. Yes, I could use the help."

"Great. I'll bring you something from Decadent Treats across the street, so you don't have to actually leave, but can take a break in the back."

And she was gone out the front door before I could say anything. She was a like a fairy godmother, offering to help and even bring food, but whether that was a good thing remained to be seen. The silver bell on the front door rang frantically. Hadn't I just removed that damn bell? I glanced at the door. Yep, it was hanging there, and for equal measure, looked underneath the counter—nope, it wasn't there. Charles was trying to tell me something—whether a warning or approval—I'd never know.

Mariah Carey clicked on, and I groaned, dropping my head into my hands.

# CHAPTER 11

I did my closing ritual, tidying up the shelves of dolls, doll accessories, miniatures, and dollhouse furniture. A child had gotten into the doll parts area and had "reorganized" the loose arms and legs, sorting them with a logic I couldn't figure out—it took me a while to fix it. It could've been worse, and I was choosing to believe the red-headed little girl truly thought she was helping. Tidying the Giving Tree, I noted how few of the paper ornaments were left. Hopefully, we'd get a lot of donations in the next few days—the donation shelves in the back room looked a bit emptier than I would've liked. I'd fill in the gaps out of my store stock if I had to. No foster child was going to wake up Christmas morning without a present, even if I had to buy toys from the big box stores thirty miles away to make it happen.

Between customers, I'd even found a few minutes to call local restaurants, trying to find one willing to cater the foster kids' holiday dinner as cheaply as possible. There were a few possibilities, though many restaurants had referenced the high cost of food and labor when I'd told them about the budget. I got it—things were getting tighter and tighter, squeezing small businesses. But I still needed to give the foster kids a wonderful holiday, and the dinner wasn't going to be pizza or hamburgers unless there was truly no other choice.

I was still waiting on a few calls back, and then I'd send the list to Daphne for her team to follow-up: I'd done my part. They could close the deal from there. Collecting a tin of cat food and Max's bowl, I went outside. I'd tried to find the cat after Lara had left, but he hadn't come out. I hadn't expected him to; it was too early for his nighttime meal, and I'd never seen him during the day. But this storm was going to be bad. A frigid breeze whipped down the alley, the air freezing in my lungs. My breath puffed out and giant flakes of snow danced through the air, landing on the already frozen cobblestones.

Oh, no. Max wouldn't survive this.

"Here kitty, kitty, kitty!" I called, my voice shaking as my teeth chattered. "Come on, kitty!" I clinked my nails against the metal can, hoping the sound would help. But the falling snow seemed to absorb it and I doubted anyone other than me could hear it. I stepped further out into the alley, wrapping my arms around my middle, shivering.

"Come on Max," I called. "I have a nice warm bed for you inside. You're going to freeze, you dummy." I went down the alley and squinted beneath the dumpster. Snow was already starting to accumulate around it. I peeked inside, rattling the lid, trying to see if I could scare him out if he was hiding underneath it.

Nothing. Not even a rat moved.

I went into the middle of the alley and looked up and down it, hands on my hips.

Nothing. No movements, no eyes glowing out of the shadows.

"Max?" I called again. "Kitty, kitty? Come on, idiot—I'm trying to keep you from dying."

Suddenly, brakes screeched in front of my store, followed by the sound of tires sliding across ice. I froze, my breath puffing out in front of me, waiting for the crash. It never came. Still holding the bowl and can of cat food, I darted out of the alley and around to the street, nearly slipping on black ice.

The businesses were closed, their windows mostly dark, so most of the light came from the streetlights. The snow was coming down harder, blanketing everything in white. A green Prius sat in the middle of the street, fishtailed. The driver's side door was open, the driver using their phone flashlight to examine the front bumper.

I recognized the dark hair and red coat. "Daphne?" I called. "Is that you? You okay?"

"I think so," she said, hunching her shoulders against the cold, snow dusting her hair. "God, I braked to avoid this black cat darting across the middle of the road and almost lost control. I thought I might have hit him."

My heart sunk. Had that been Max? I inspected her bumper. No damage, no blood, no little black body in the street. Hopefully, she'd missed him.

"Max?" I called out.

"Was that your cat? You should keep him inside!"

"He's a stray," I explained. "I just feed him sometimes. I haven't been able to actually bring him inside my store. Hell, I don't even know his actual name. I just call him Max. Here, kitty, kitty!"

"If you name a cat, it's yours."

"We can talk semantics later. Let's just try to find him. He won't survive this storm." We rustled the bushes, hoping to scare him out. We froze when we heard a growly meow from within a bush. Shivering so hard my back and knees hurt, I slowly approached.

"I think he's in there," Daphne said. She unwound a glittery Christmas scarf and draped it around my neck. "You're going to freeze."

She was right; I was wearing nothing more than a pair of jeans and a sweater. "Thank you," I said. "I'm glad you're okay."

"Me too," Daphne said. "Let's get your cat because he'll freeze too."

"Here, Max," I called, opening the can of food and setting it in front of the bush. I tucked my hands into my armpits, trying to keep them warm while we waited to see if he'd come out. With a rustle and a distrustful glance, he approached the food and began to lap it up. Thank God he didn't take too long. Poor thing must have been starving.

"Now what?" Daphne whispered. "If we try to grab him, he'll bolt."

"I got it," I said, unwinding the scarf. Saying a quick prayer, and mentally promising to buy Daphne another scarf, I threw it over the black cat. Rather than running, he dropped to the ground, and I scooped him up. Max struggled a little, then relaxed into my arms. The poor thing must be half-frozen.

"You got him," she whispered.

I cradled him close, feeling him tremble. "Poor thing," I said. "I gotta get him inside. If you come by the store tomorrow, I'll give you your scarf back."

"Oh, don't worry about it," she said. "I don't like that scarf, anyway."

A car came up behind hers and beeped its horn, the headlights illuminating the falling snow. The driver rolled down the window. "You two okay? Need a tow truck?" It was Patrick, likely heading home after closing his store. Of all the people it could've been. The universe and I were long overdue for a conversation.

"We're good," Daphne called to him. "We were just rescuing this cat. But I'll move my car out of the way and let Kayla get inside."

I showed him the creature shivering in my arms, while Daphne climbed into her car, straightened and drove off with a quick wave.

But instead of following her, Patrick got out of his car. "Why do you have my cat?" he asked. "And how did he get out here?"

## CHAPTER 12

"Your cat?" I asked, the scarf-wrapped bundle in my arms burrowing into me. I trembled as snowflakes stuck to my eyelashes and covered my shoulders. "Max is your cat?"

"I think that cat is mine," Patrick clarified, squinting to get a better look at him. I swung away, trying to protect Max and keep him warm. There was no way this cat was Patrick's. It was a stray I'd been feeding for months. "Let's go into your shop, Kayla," he said. "We can talk more there; you're going to freeze if we stay talking out here. I just need to move my car out of the street."

How could Max be his cat? There must be more than one black stray around here. How would he even know Max was his cat? And since when did he have a cat? Maybe I should text Lara and ask. *Your brother is claiming the stray cat I've been feeding for months is yours. Does your brother even have a cat, or is he trying to steal mine?* Yeah, that didn't sound crazy. Not at all.

"Come around the back," I said. "The front door's locked."

Clutching the cat to my chest, I went into the alley. The snow was letting up, but my shivers were getting worse, and thank God, Max wasn't trying to get away. I wasn't sure I'd be able to hold him if he suddenly tried to jump from my arms.

I gasped when I went into the lighted warmth of my backroom. It felt like a sauna in here compared to the outside. Closing the door behind me, I set Max on the floor, expecting him to bolt under the desk. But he didn't. He just stayed crouching, frozen in fear. In the last three months of feeding him, I'd never managed to get him into my store. Cooing, "You're ok, I'm just going to unwrap you. You're okay," over and over, I tugged the glittery Christmas scarf free. He was damp with snow and cold to the touch. He didn't move as I petted him. "Good kitty," I said. "How about some more food?" But before I could get another can, Patrick came through the back door, letting in a burst of cold air. Max took advantage of my distraction to bolt away to hide under my desk. I let him go. He couldn't get into much in here—it was just boxes of toys. And the heater was close to him; he'd be okay once he warmed up.

I hoped.

"I've been looking everywhere for him," Patrick said. "What happened? How'd you find him?"

"Are you sure that's your cat?" I asked. "There's many black cats out in the world and I've been feeding this one for three months."

"Does he have a little white toe on his left front paw and a scarred ear?"

Hell. "Hard to say," I said, stalling. "We'll have to check."

He frowned, likely knowing I was lying. "So, you've been the one feeding him? I mean, I knew someone was—he kept getting out and coming back fatter and fatter. And how did

Daphne get involved? And why were you both in the middle of the street looking for him?"

"I think she almost hit him," I said, crossing my arms against my chest. "I was out back and heard the screech of brakes and went out to see what happened. She said he went running across the street and braked to avoid him. There's black ice everywhere." My shivering was getting worse despite the building's heat as my body tried to warm back up. Patrick draped my coat around my shoulders, rubbing my arms. I was so cold, I could feel the warmth of his hands through my sweater. For an instant, I wanted nothing more than to curl into him, let him wrap his arms around me.

I looked up at him, startled by the emotion, and he smiled at me, a quirky side-grin. "I can't stand to see someone so cold," he said. "But it's warm in here and you'll warm up quick."

I stepped back, and Patrick dropped his hands. This man thought toys were disposable, and his toy store was just there to make money, I reminded myself. "How is Max your cat?" I demanded.

"First, his name is Ichabod."

What the hell? "Ichabod?"

"It's from the Legend of Sleepy Hollow," Patrick said, his green eyes sparkling with laughter. "Gramps wanted a spooky name for a black cat." He looked around my backroom at the shelves arranged by dolls, accessories, and dollhouses, everything well organized so I could find it at a moment's notice. "I wouldn't have expected it was you feeding him," he continued.

What did that mean? Was I not the type of person who would feed a stray cat? "Why?"

"You just seem more like a dog person." He leaned close to a box, reading the label. "Do you really sell a lot of dollhouse furniture? Not the plastic, brightly colored kind, but the more old-fashioned ones?"

I couldn't keep up with this conversation. "I do fine, thank you." I was getting warmer, my shivers decreasing. I'd known the cat was too fat to be a true stray, but I'd liked the feeling of caring for someone. Of someone counting on me. I'd missed it since Luke and his new family had moved away. Now I felt ridiculous. Of course, Ma—Ichabod had belonged to someone.

"So, you were his second family," Patrick said, turning away from my inventory and rocking back on his heels. "I've had to put him on a diet, which he hates and now he yowls and knocks over everything in the house." He gave the desk a pointed stare, but Max/Ichabod didn't respond. "He's getting so fat."

"No family," I said without thinking. "Just me." Patrick's face changed, but I didn't have the energy to interpret it. I shifted a box on a shelf behind him, straightening it and lining it up with the rest. "Why do you let him out? He would've frozen tonight and there's coyotes in the hills. And he could've gotten hit by a car." I shouldn't have been asking, but I still hadn't had lunch and now dinner seemed far away, though it was just now eight.

"It's not my choice," Patrick said. "He's brilliant, and Gramps always let him do whatever he wanted. I've been trying to keep him inside the house, but he knows how to open the window on the second floor. And it doesn't matter how I try to block him from it, he still manages to get to it." He pushed his glasses up his nose.

I wondered if Max was getting out, trying to find his prior owner, missing him and not understanding that Patrick's grandfather was gone. That made my heart hurt. Poor Max.

The cat let out a grumble-howl under the desk.

"I'll get him and take him home," Patrick said. "Let me know if you spot him again, and please don't feed him. He really is too fat."

Patrick bent over and Max—Ichabod, let out a low hiss and swiped, claws out. "Dang-it," Patrick said, sticking his finger in a mouth. "I'm trying to help you."

"Let me try," I said, squatting and holding my hand out. After staring at me, Max came out from under the desk, meowing. He began to twine around my legs, rubbing his cheeks against my jeans. I picked him up, the cat purring madly. Resisting the urge to give him a goodbye kiss, I passed him over to Patrick. The purring stopped, but he seemed docile, head-butting Patrick instead of scratching him.

"Oh, I see," Patrick said. "You're nicer around Kayla, aren't you?"

Something in my heart broke. He wasn't mine to cuddle. Not anymore. The plans I had for the future floated away. He'd never sleep in the backroom, peeking out to say hello to special customers.

"I won't feed him anymore," I murmured. "Here," I said, moving toward the shelf I kept Ichabod's supplies on. "I've got his food and bowl. I even bought him a cat bed. Let me box it up for you."

"Oh, that's okay," Patrick said. "He's got plenty."

Of course he did. My eyes filled with tears, and I blinked them away before Patrick could see them. "Seriously. I don't have a need for them."

"This cat is a grumpy old man. If he was coming to see you, he's not going to stop just because you give me his bed. We may have to split custody." He smiled fondly down at the cat.

I petted Ichabod's head. He closed his eyes and purred,

head-butting my fingers. "Thanks for finding him," Patrick murmured. "He might have died tonight, and I don't think I could've handled that too."

The tears weren't going away, no matter how much I blinked. "He's a good kitty," I said, continuing to stroke the soft head as Ichabod increased his purr. It was just a cat. I should be happy he wasn't going to freeze in the snow like I'd feared. "I'll let you out the front—it's closer to your car."

I walked with Patrick into my store, and he turned slowly, taking in the chandelier, sparkly concrete floor, and holiday decorations, the faint scent of cypress drifting over all of it; in the evening, with the lights twinkling, it oozed Christmas cheer. "I've been meaning to pick your brain about how you did all this. It's incredible. Did you hire a designer?"

I shrugged, feeling so emotionally drained I couldn't take any pride in his compliment. "I did work with someone to draw up the plans. But I did a lot of the work myself."

"Do you have a background in art? How much did this—" Ichabod squirmed in Patrick's arms. "We'll have to talk later. I've got some ideas to run by you, get your thoughts on since you seem to be so good at this. Maybe over coffee tomorrow?" Patrick asked with that side-grin. "I can give you an update on this guy."

I didn't have the energy to pick apart the subtext. "Not right now," I said. "It's the holidays and I'm so tired by the time I'm done with work."

"Got it," Patrick said. "After the holidays, then. And thanks for taking care of my cat for so long."

"Not a problem," I murmured. Then I closed the door behind them, locking it and turning off the lights, so it was just me and the holiday twinkle. I watched Patrick get into his car, his lips moving in what was obviously a one-sided conversation with Ma—Ichabod. Despite myself, I smiled—just a little—watching him scold the cat, who was probably crouching in the backseat, ignoring him. Maybe Patrick wasn't so bad after all; not if he cared for Ichabod so much. I turned around and looked at my shop, seeking the Giving Tree, and cheerful decorations that normally gave me so much joy. But not tonight. Losing Max/Ichabod, even if it was to someone who obviously cared for him, had left a hole in my heart.

## CHAPTER 13

The next morning, the sun shone clean and clear; the snowstorm having blanketed the town in ice and crystal and turning Penduline Village into a real-life Christmas card. Knowing people from the city thirty miles away would come to see the Christmas decor all coated in snow, city workers began as early as eight, dusting snow off trees, and de-icing the streets while businesses prepared for the onslaught of tourists. As it was the Sunday after Thanksgiving, Santa and his elves got ready for the long lines in the old-timey "Santa's workshop" and enterprising children prepared to sell hot chocolate and candy canes to those waiting.

And by ten, the tourists had come in droves, causing traffic jams in Old Towne and minor fender benders in the neighborhoods as the tourists parked in front of people's homes. By one, Decadent Treats had run out of breads, cookies, cinnamon, and sticky rolls and the specialty gift store next door to mine had to put in a rush order for holiday scarves and hats from their distributors.

And the snow didn't melt, but stayed, glistening and turning our town into a social media Christmas Mecca. During that week I worked twelve-hour days and after the first day, didn't know what I'd do without Lara. As agreed, she brought me lunch the first day, and seeing the line of people waiting for gift wrapping, never left. She stayed to work the cash register, upselling the small impulse purchases I kept there while I wrapped presents, brought merchandise out of the back room, unlocked the case with the collectable dolls and generally answered questions. When things slowed down, she'd stay, working the cash register so I could package online orders and contact my distributors for more merchandise. Then the next day she'd show up at eight a.m. to help me restock, tidy, and prepare for the day. She didn't leave until after five and never once complained about her feet hurting. Lara was fun too, with a wide smile and an easy laugh, joking about silly things without being mean or picking on the customers. I sensed Charles liked her too, unlike Franklin. Charles never nudged or swooped past her, frightening her.

And with her working the cash register, I could do the thing I loved most; helping customers find their perfect doll, doll accessory, or dollhouse. I loved answering questions about building and furnishing the dollhouses. Loved to assist people when they were looking for a doll part or trying to find a wig or eyeballs for a doll they were restoring. Loved taking the time to explain the value behind the Barbies in the collectible case and point out the extensive and detailed costumes on the Madame Alexanders. The woman with the turquoise gloves came back, purchasing the Madame Alexander Scarlett in the green velvet dress and a large dollhouse kit I never would've sold to her without Lara's encouragement. I even had a chance for a long conversation with an older English woman about the vintage Queen Elizabeth's Coronation doll I had, hearing how much the royal family had meant to her; eventually I sold the doll to her for several thousand dollars.

All was busy, chaotic, and perfect. I'd even heard from Franklin—his parents were doing okay and would soon be out of the hospital. But he was going to stay with them until after Christmas. Thank God for Lara; Franklin could stay with his parents and help his sister with no guilt.

About a week after the snowstorm, I was on a stepladder dusting Barbies on a tall shelf when I heard a customer say, "I think the toy store on Third Street has these too." She pointed at a Fashion Dream Doll. "And they're cheaper there. Heck, cheaper than online stores, if you can believe that."

"Yeah, there's some sort of special," her friend said, tugging off her gloves to pull her phone out of a back pocket. "I think I saw it on Instagram." She swiped up. "Yep. Cheaper, with free gift wrapping and an extra outfit."

"Excuse me," I said. "I'm so sorry to interrupt, but were you saying that these dolls are available at the toy store on Third Street? Toys and Games?" Anger churned in my chest. Was Patrick intentionally undercutting me?

The women gave me an odd look. "I'm sorry," I said, carefully stepping down the ladder, so I wasn't looking down at them. "I just want to know if I run out or they have a Fashion Dream model I don't have. I can send the customer over there." The women exchanged glances and the one with the phone stuffed it back into her pocket. They knew I was lying. Hell, I probably sounded insane. "I just watched the old black-and-white Miracle on 34th Street," I babbled, trying to save the moment. "Remember, there's that scene where Santa tells the parents to shop at Gimbels, though he works for Macy's, and he almost gets fired for doing that. But he says all that matters is the kids, not where the toy came from." I gave a one-shoulder shrug, trying to seem like I cared about the kids more than sounding deranged. "It's like that," I clarified. "I just need to know if he's selling dolls because he hasn't done that before. And it's not a big deal. All that matters are the children." Oh God, now I was quoting the movie verbatim.

"Thanks for your assistance," one woman said as they hurried from the store without answering my question. Or purchasing anything, but that was secondary.

Well, they weren't any help. Pulling out my phone, I clicked over to Instagram, finding Patrick's store. Sure enough, there was an ad for the Fashion Dream Dolls, including blinking animation advertising free wrapping AND an outfit with the purchase of a doll. AND the cost for all of that was five dollars less than my cheapest version of a single Fashion Doll.

Five dollars! What the hell? Dolls were mine! We had unspoken rules. He took care of the puzzles, the Legos, the board games, the Nerf guns, the science experiments, and I had dolls, and other dollish stuff. Patrick had never stocked anything more than the occasional Barbie or baby doll, all basic for those stopping in to buy something else. Even the tourists skipped his store to buy the dolls from mine. After all, he could draw from a wider range of toys and mine was limited. Specialized.

Nausea swam in my belly. My cheeks got hot as my anger rose.

He thought toys were disposable and was obviously just in this business for the money. He said we were on different sides of the toy debate, but then went ahead and stocked the one toy that mattered most to children, the one toy that children cared for, loved and imagined with the most—dolls.

Patrick had to be doing it to compete with me. He thought he could cut into my business!

Lara came in from where she'd gone to get us coffee, her hands full with two to-go cups and a bag from Decadent Treats dangling between her fingers. "I think I had to fight off a family of tourists for the last two sticky buns," she said, setting the cups down on the counter and smiling at a little girl and her mother admiring the Madame Alexander dolls in the case. "Let me know if you want to look at them any closer," she said. "They're unique, but a great way for little girls to get into doll collecting."

Was Lara actually a spy? Was she helping her brother compete with my store, telling him the prices and what I'd ordered versus what was in stock? Was that why she'd been so nice to me, helping and working the cash register? So her brother could compete with me?

But we weren't competitors. Not really. Yes, Patrick and I sold toys, but ... we were completely different from each other.

Lara sipped at her coffee, watching the little girl and her mother ohhh and awww over the dolls, noticing all the details on a Comic-Con exclusive Monster High, including the gems in her dress and the little cat that came with the doll. "You okay?" she asked me when I didn't come over to collect my coffee.

"No," I said, my voice hoarse. I was being ridiculous, right? Lara wasn't a spy. She was a fairy godmother.

"What's wrong?" she asked. "Do you need a break?"

The silver bell on the front door jangled, and I glanced at it, seeing nothing there. Charles was expressing his opinion, but I had no idea what that was.

"Why are you helping me?" I asked her.

## CHAPTER 14

I crossed the store to Lara, so angry my hands shook. "Are you spying for your brother?" I hissed, trying to be mindful of the customers.

"No, of course not," she said, her green eyes going wide with shock. "I haven't talked to him, other than like did-you-want-eggs-this-morning, for a few days. He's been working in the basement at Gramp's house, and I hate that room. Why would you think I am?"

"This," I said, shoving my phone with the Instagram ad for her brother's store in her face. "He's charging less than me for the same dolls, with free gift wrapping. AND a free outfit. Dolls are mine. This is a doll store. It's not a general toy store with Legos and Nerf and board games like his store. And it gets worse. He thinks toys are disposable. Why is he advertising he has specialty dolls, of all things!"

The little girl's mother eyed us and moved away from the doll case, shuffling her daughter down an aisle. Guess I wasn't being very Christmasy right now.

"Come here," I said, drawing Lara into the back room, but

keeping the door open so I could see the cash register in case anyone wanted to buy anything.

Lara untwisted the scarf from around her neck, dropping it onto the desk and said, "Let me look. I don't know what he's been up to." She took my phone and started scrolling. "I didn't even know Patrick had an Instagram or knew how to do ads." She swiped up. "Okay, so it looks like he has a ton of ads and that he's offering a bunch of specials on dolls and accessories. I didn't know he had stocked dolls. He always said Legos were where he made his money."

"He's never had dolls," I said between my teeth. "It's this unspoken rule between us. I have dolls, doll accessories, miniatures, dollhouses, and dollhouse furniture; he has everything else. I've never said anything when he's stocked the occasional Barbie or baby doll—I get it—impulse buys for his customers who suddenly remember they need another present or the occasional child that just MUST have that Barbie. But the Fashion Dream Dolls are different—those are in immense demand by kids who love dolls. He's just trying to make money off of people's wishes, not because he believes in a child's imagination. "

"I hear you," she said, her voice soft.

"And he's undercutting me, too. That has to be intentional. He's advertising the doll is five dollars cheaper than mine AND the free doll clothes AND free gift wrapping! Somehow, he knows my prices."

"Well, we do offer free gift wrapping, too," Lara said. "But I haven't talked to him about your prices, I swear. They're up on your website, right?"

"I guess." Okay, that was a good point. "But he—"

"Kayla, I've done nothing but help you these last few days because I love your store and you're struggling trying to run this place by yourself during Christmas." She held my eyes with hers. "I have told him how amazing your store is, and how we have lines out the door for people to buy your toys. Maybe he saw an opportunity, but I wasn't intentionally spying or anything. I love what your store stands for."

"Stands for?" I asked.

"You tell people everyone deserves a doll. Deserves a toy they love more than anything. Deserves something to take care of, to love. Everyone, not every little girl, but EVERYONE. I've seen you work compassionately with little boys looking for a stuffed animal or a doll to dress up. I've seen you talk with that one woman who comes in and buys doll parts for therapy dolls for her clients who are hurting and trying to heal. You're amazing with that boy who comes in with autism. I've watched you take the time to play in the dollhouses with a little girl who insisted a hippogriff and bats live in them, rearranging the furniture to accommodate her imaginary creatures. And then the little girl left, buying nothing, and you had to put it all back. Your store is amazing, and it allows children a chance to play and dream when their time is getting sucked away by the internet and schedules. Your store is rare and precious. And no, my brother doesn't get that."

"Thank you," I said, slightly mollified. "But Patrick shouldn't be selling dolls like the Fashion Dream ones. And he shouldn't be undercutting me. If I decided to sell the Lego Friends collection, I would've told him. It's unprofessional that he didn't talk to me." If I'd been twelve years old, I would've folded my arms against my chest and stuck out my lower lip. Instead, I glared over Lara's shoulder.

Lara peeked out the door and saw a line forming at the counter. "I say you go and yell at him," she said. "I got the store. Get it out of your system. He needs to hear it from you."

God, that sounded so good. And I hadn't seen his store in a while—I could see what he was selling; maybe I'd start stocking it too. See how he felt about competing with an actual toy store and not ... a store that just wanted to make money and didn't care about the kids.

## CHAPTER 15

Snatching my jacket and beanie off the desk chair in the storage room, I headed out the back door, walking the few blocks over to Patrick's store. Like all our businesses in Old Towne, his was in a converted building, and had started life as a general store. It'd been various boutiques and even a Jazzercise at one point. I'd always coveted this building with its tall glass windows and brick exterior. I could imagine setting up an amazing display within that would speak to the imagination and joy of children; something that would make tourists, walking by, stop, and want to come inside. But Patrick kept his windows clear, showing just the boring inside of his store—shelves full of stacked and boxed toys. He obviously assumed his store's placement—right as tourists came into Old Towne would be enough to bring in the shoppers. It also helped his store was the only general toy store in Penduline Village, and anyone wanting Batman figurines or board games had to buy from him, order online, or drive the thirty miles to the city of Bisham.

The icy breeze and slushy snow had cooled my temper by the time I got to Patrick's. It wasn't like me to get so worked up; it had to be the stress of holidays and planning the foster kids' dinner. Was it really that big of a deal that he was selling the same specialty dolls I did? I had cornered the market on dolls in this town and had tourists driving for hundreds of miles to come to my store, not his. There was even that write up in the New York Times, lest one forget. Or a mention, which was the same as a write up. And stomping over to his store to yell at him wouldn't change anything. He could sell what he wanted; I wasn't in charge of the world.

But maybe I would stock some Legos—they had some new ones catered to girls that would fit into my store's motif well. I'd almost decided to turn around and go back, save my energy for my customers, but when I got to his store, I saw a temporary chalkboard sign out in front, designed to lure shoppers in.

*Fashion Dream Dolls in stock. Unique specialty accessories. Cheap! Perfect for that little girl on your shopping list.*

Beneath it was the special posted on Instagram: the Fashion Dream Doll, five dollars cheaper than I offered, along with the promise of the free outfit and gift wrapping.

My face flushed. This was direct competition. He could've done me the courtesy of telling me he was going to offer the specialty dolls in his store. I mean, I couldn't stop him from selling them, but why would he start now? Why after seeing my store, after his sister came to work for me, would he suddenly think, 'I've got a great idea! I should sell dolls!'

There was no way it was a coincidence. And he didn't even wait until after Christmas! He knew how hard it was to turn a profit as a toy store owner and decided to cut into mine.

I stepped inside, my blood boiling, and froze. What the heck was going on here? He'd remodeled ... maybe? But it didn't make any sense. There was a gigantic robotic ... something in the middle of the store with industrial looking tracks running across the twelve-foot ceiling. Those must have been expensive to put up. The robotic ... thing took up most of the room in the first third of the store and was dark gray steel with lots of joints. It was protected from any children by the clear plastic that reminded me of the barriers stores had put up between workers and shoppers during COVID. I'd been so happy to toss those in the dumpster the first chance I had. Someone had hung a sign in bright colors on the plastic that said, "Mr. ToyDrop." As I stood there, I watched an action figure in its plastic container shoot across the ceiling track and halt behind the robotic arm. The robotic arm swung into motion, lifting the action figure from the track, heading toward a container where a little boy waited, hopping slightly in place. Ah ... the toy was going to drop into the box. For crying out loud, the name of the robot wasn't even clever. The arm hovered, then let out a wrenching sound, freezing, the action figure still clutched in its grip. Red lights flickered on, and an alarm went off—a loud: WHOOP, WHOOP, WHOOP.

Holy cow, that was loud! I resisted the urge to put my hands over my ears.

"Ahhhhh ... shoot," the boy shouted. "Mom, it broke again."

"Yeah, I noticed," the mom said between whoops, looking toward the counter where a college-aged student was ringing up guests. She rolled her eyes.

"Be right there," he yelled over the alarm. "Let me turn it off first."

He tapped on his screen, winced, then grimaced. "Hang on," he called. "I have to restart the system."

Patrick came out from the back office and went over to inspect the robotic arm. Pulling keys from his pocket, he unlocked the plastic barrier and pressed a button on the robot. The alarm stopped, and the arm swung back into motion, dropping the action figure into the box. The container whooshed open, and the boy could grab the toy.

"Okay," the mom said, guiding the boy and his action figure toward the counter. "We're not doing that again. We're just going to get this and figure out presents for your other cousins later."

"I can help," Patrick said. "Are you looking for more action figures? Or maybe a board game? Or I got it—dolls! The Fashion Dream Dolls are on sale."

Oh hell no. Tell me he didn't just go there.

The mom pulled out her phone, checked the time and winced. "We do need more action figures. But I don't think we have time; we're already running late for our time slot with Santa."

"Action figures are aisle 3," Patrick said. "You don't need to use Mr. ToyDrop. Just grab what you want and bring them to the counter."

"Okay," Mom said. "Let's go quick. You have five minutes to pick out four toys. God knows going online will take the same amount of time." They disappeared down an aisle made up of wire shelves with stacks of dusty boxed toys.

"Hey Kayla," Patrick said, his eyes lighting up. "What do you think?" He jerked a thumb at the robot. "Just got this for Christmas." He looked up at Mr. ToyDrop. "Something different; make the store stand out like yours does, and I mean, kids love robots."

They did actually, but only if they worked right and parents didn't get annoyed. And it seemed like the maintenance of it would be a pain.

The lights on the robot blinked out. "Damn it," Patrick muttered and reached behind the robot to hang a well-used Out-of-Order sign. "Still working out the kinks, but I got a great deal on it from this store that went out of business. I'm thinking of totally revolutionizing this place. You know, using technology, making it sleek and modern as a counterpoint to how whimsical yours is."

That actually wasn't a terrible idea and was a better one than having wire shelves full of dusty toys.

"So, what are you doing here?" Patrick asked. "Taking me up on my coffee offer? I hear Lara is working with you full time now. She loves your store."

Before I could say anything, a dad stepped over to ask Patrick a question. "I saw your special for the Fashion Dream Dolls ... I just need to grab one."

"Oh yes," Patrick said. "They're on that table." He jerked his thumb to a folding table with a crooked pink tablecloth and dolls stacked haphazardly. I rolled my eyes. Looked like there were only three varieties of outfits; all basic dresses, the cheapest a store owner could get. He hadn't even bothered to stock pants or the more unique outfits for the Fashion Dream Dolls, like the unicorn onesie parents had formed a line around my store to purchase a few months ago.

Seriously?

"That's actually what I wanted to talk to you about," I said. "You're selling dolls now?"

"I am!" he said with a big smile. "You gave me the idea!"

Wait what? "I did?"

"Yeah, you were talking about how important toys are to kids, how a lot of kids don't think they're disposable and how some toys, like dolls, are important to kids' development. I mean, I'm not sure I agree, but I can see how for SOME kids, dolls might be important. Lara's been telling me how busy your store is, which I couldn't believe. I didn't think anyone bought dolls anymore. But the Fashion dolls are flying off the table, which is really going to help offset—"

"My store sells dolls. Yours gets everything else. Why would you start selling dolls now?"

"Well, I just—"

"And you're undercutting me." I pointed my finger at the table. "No wonder they're flying off the shelves. Yours are five dollars cheaper WITH a free outfit?"

"Well, I had—"

"Why don't you just focus on selling Legos and Nerf guns? You could do a special with that and undercut the big box stores. My store doesn't sell that stuff, and yours does. Or maybe I'll start selling the Lego Friend collection! It would go great in my store, and my distributor recommended it." I tried to keep my voice down, tried not to cause a scene. "But I didn't because I knew you sold Legos and I didn't want to compete with you! It's hard enough to turn a profit with online and big box stores undercutting us as it is. And rent, electricity, and hell, even food is getting more and more expensive. Taylor's bakery is up to $17.00 for a cup of soup and a sandwich!"

## WRAPPING PAPER RIVALS

Patrick's shoulders dropped, and he stared down at the ground. "I know. It's getting bad and ... I'm struggling too. But ... I wasn't thinking about competing with you," he mumbled. "I just need—"

"I know you didn't think," I said, my words coming fast and hard. The people in line for the cash register were turning to look at us. But I couldn't stop. "Your store is a general toy store; the name is Toys and Games for crying out loud. My store is THE specialty store for dolls in this area for hundreds of miles! If you want to specialize, specialize in puzzles or board games or something! Leave me the dolls."

I stomped away before he could answer, slamming outside to the snowy sidewalk. Why? Why would he not think of my store? Why would he start selling dolls? And why was there a robotic arm in the middle of his store? He couldn't be hurting for money—even used—that robot would've cost several thousand dollars. No wonder he could afford to undercut me.

The icy wind cooled my heated cheeks as I ran the conversation over in my mind; anxiety, anger, and embarrassment churning in my stomach. I'd won that, right? He knew I had dolls, and he had everything else, right? He knew that not checking with me was wrong, right?

I headed back to my store, unsettled. He hadn't argued; in fact, he'd seemed to agree with me. So why wasn't I feeling powerful? Instead, I just felt ... sad. Patrick had looked so defeated when I'd yelled at him. But he had to be doing fine. Right? Before I knew it, I was back in the alley behind my store. I looked at the dumpster Max used to hide beneath, missing the damn cat. Hell, this time of year was supposed to be the most amazing, but this year had been stressful and unsettling. I couldn't wait for Christmas to be over, and that wasn't like me. At least I still had Christmas day with Luke and his family to look forward to.

My phone buzzed, and I pulled it out as I slipped through the back door of my store. My screen was lit up with my son's name and picture.

## CHAPTER 16

"Luke! I was just thinking about you. You don't normally call me during the day. Everything okay?" I glanced through the door at the cash register. Like Patrick's store, the line was long, children held firmly in hand by their parents, or spinning, dancing, or just jumping throughout the store. Lara needed help. Something was going to get broken.

"I have bad news," Luke said. "My boss says I can't take the Christmas time off. He says I don't have seniority, and my coworker has all this family drama, and he's going to go and see them and if I don't stay there's not enough—"

"But he'd said he approved it."

"He said it looked good. That's why I bought refundable plane tickets—just in case."

"That's too bad," I said, fighting to keep my voice from showing disappointment. A tear traced down my cheek and I wiped it away with a gloved finger. Holding the phone against my shoulder, I struggled out of my gloves, jacket, and hat. "But I get it," I said, putting all my energy into keeping my voice steady.

"I know Mom, I'm so sorry." His voice cracked a bit. "It's just ... this is a new job and I'm still trying to prove myself. And then it's the sick time of year between the flu and COVID, so everyone keeps calling out, and nothing is getting done. We could fly out after work on Christmas Eve, but it's a long flight from Arizona to Connecticut and work is open on December 26th. We'd have to fly back Christmas night, and that's hard on Ivy and with plane tickets being so much, I'd want to fly out when we can spend a few days with you, not just one."

"I totally understand your logic," I said, fighting through my sticky emotions to get the words out, fighting to sound cheerful and supportive. It wasn't his fault, I thought as another tear ran down my cheek and I breathed shallowly to keep from sniffing into the phone. His reasoning made sense, but I couldn't believe how disappointed I was. I'd been eager to show Ivy and Tara my toy store, though Ivy was a complete science-nerd, preferring science kits, microscopes, and experiments to dolls. Now I'd have to ship the telescope I'd bought for her rather than watching her open it on Christmas morning. I wouldn't get to spend the nights before she left exploring the stars with her.

My plans floated up and away, like a torn-up love letter, released into the wind.

"But you never know," Luke continued. "I'm still working on my boss. Any chance you could come to us?"

I shook my head, then realized he couldn't see it. "Not with the store around Christmas. Franklin had a family emergency and had to be with his family. I have a volunteer helping, but I can't ask her to work on Christmas Eve or the day after Christmas. Last year, Christmas Eve was one of my top days as people bought those last-minute gifts. I can't afford to close and lose the revenue. I'm sorry."

"Totally expected," Luke said. "I know Christmas sales keep you going the rest of the year."

"But maybe once Franklin's back..." I said, talking out loud. I'd been so looking forward to seeing him and his family. "Maybe I'll get through the Christmas returns and sale of leftover stock and then come see you. Maybe we could have New Year's Eve together and celebrate Christmas a few days late." There was a crash from inside the store, and I stuck my head out from the back room. Someone had knocked over a few boxes of Barbies. I breathed a quick sigh of relief that it wasn't one of the dollhouses.

"I'll be right there," I whisper-called to Lara, showing her I was on the phone.

"Ummm ... yeah ... coming to us on New Year's could work," Luke said. I heard a quick muffled conversation.

"Why wouldn't that work?" I asked.

"Well ... we only have the one guest room and Tara's family is staying with us for New Year's. There's like four people already crammed into that room. I think probably Tara's sister will end up sleeping on the couch."

"Got it." They had no room for me. And couldn't make room.

"I'm sorry," Luke said. "I didn't even think you coming to see us was a possibility with the store, or I would've offered that."

But he'd just asked—I pushed down annoyance. It wasn't his fault, it wasn't his fault, it wasn't his fault, I chanted to myself. He had another family with other obligations now. He couldn't drop everything for me. And shouldn't.

"Of course," I said, trying to stay cordial and wiping away

another tear. I had to pull it together. Lara needed me and I couldn't be crying in front of the customers. "Totally get it."

"But we're going to take some time to come and see you. I promise. How does February sound?"

It sounded like any other month; nothing special about it. Except for a made-up Hallmark holiday for lovers—something I didn't have and had given up on. I tried to reframe my thoughts. It actually might be nice to distract myself from the lovey-dovey holiday with family functions. And the store would be much slower; I could have Franklin watch the store and truly take some time with Luke's family.

"That sounds good." I tried to push some good will into my voice, though I couldn't seem to stop the tears from flowing. "I can't wait. Send me the dates and I'll make sure everything is ready for the three of you. I have to go—the line is crazy here."

"Thank you, mom, for being so understanding," Luke said. "I think if you'd cried, I would've figured it out and I don't have any idea how to do that. But I know how much Christmas and family mean to you and it sucks we won't be able to spend it together."

I wiped away an errant tear, fighting to wall up my emotions. Hell, I might need to call my therapist. "Totally get it," I said. "It's not your fault, and there will be other Christmases."

I hung up the phone and took ten deep breaths, feeling calmer and more centered by the time I was done. I would deal with Luke's news this evening. Not in front of Lara or my customers. Patting my cheeks to get rid of any more errant tears, I slipped through the back door. Like Patrick's store, the line at the cash register was five people deep, and I relieved Lara from where she was trying to professionally, but quickly wrap several Barbies.

"How'd it go?" she asked.

There was no way she could've known about Luke and my brain stuttered until I realized she was asking about Patrick. Hell, had I gone to confront him only fifteen minutes ago?

"Fine," I said as breezily as I could, though embarrassment flooded through me. Why had I even gone over to his store to yell at him? That wasn't like me. "I don't know," I said. "I mean, I confronted him, and he said he wasn't thinking when he ordered the Fashion Dream Dolls."

"He wasn't," Lara confirmed. "But I don't think his store is doing well, not as well as yours is, at least."

"But there was this robot—"

Lara snorted and then smiled at the next customer, managing to chat with me and ring up a dad, his arms full of baby dolls. "Don't get me started on the robot (that'll be $36.89, including tax). He just bought that because he enjoys tinkering. And he's jealous."

"Of what?" I asked, curling glittery red and green ribbon and handing off brightly wrapped presents with a smile.

"Of this." She waved her hand around at my décor. "He was telling me he wants his store to be like yours, only with technology. Sleek and modern (hello! What are you buying today?)"

"He told me that, too. But dolls don't play into his brand."

"Yeah. My brother is an idiot. However, he really does love that store."

I shook my head. "There's no way. He thinks toys are disposable."

Lara shrugged and gave me a small smile. "He has his reasons for wanting to own a toy store. But they're his—not mine. Don't you have the foster kids' dinner meeting in a few minutes? I'm surprised you came back here."

I glanced at my watch. Son-of-a—I did. I'd totally forgotten about the meeting. And Patrick was going to be there too. This was going to be awkward.

I pretended to sneeze into my shoulder. "Achoo! Looks like I can't go. Coming down with something. Don't want to get everyone sick."

Lara playfully rolled her eyes. "You're fine."

"But your brother is going to be there," I hissed and then smiled at the next customer.

"Then you shouldn't have gone and yelled at him. Is this for you or for a friend?" Lara said to the little girl stepping forward with a Monster High doll.

"You encouraged me," I muttered.

"Go," Lara said. "You're going to be late. And oh—" Lara lowered her voice and leaned over. "We need to talk about your ghost, when you come back. She's making me mad."

That was just one more thing I couldn't handle. Without saying a word, I went into the back, grabbed my jacket and cold weather accessories, putting my hand on the doorknob to the alley. "Charles," I hissed. "Please behave until I get back. I can't do this without her!"

# CHAPTER 17

City Hall was only a few blocks away, but my mind refused to settle, bouncing between my argument with Patrick, Luke's bad news, and fears that my ghost would chase away Lara. God, what else could go wrong today?

And why did I keep asking that, tempting the universe? I knew better.

Stopping in front of City Hall, I pulled out my phone and started a text to Daphne.

> Hey you. My store is super busy today and I'm going to have to miss the meeting.

It wasn't a full lie. I owned a toy store, and it was less than two weeks 'til Christmas. Busy was an understatement. I was pulling in record sales both in person and online. And not sleeping. Or really eating unless Lara put food in my hands.

The three dots appeared, and I waited for her response.

> I can see you standing outside. Get in here. We've got lots to do.

> Just text me what you need.

> I shouldn't have left my store. It's a crazy day, and this isn't fair to my assistant.

Who I wasn't even paying and was depending purely on the goodness of her heart. God, I was taking so much advantage of her.

> Come out of the cold.

> Besides, I don't have the time to tell you separately what we're talking about in the meeting. It's too much work to summarize the plans when I'm already overwhelmed. And we've got a ton more help than last meeting. I found some interns who needed hours and some of the other business owners are here.

Trying to think of another excuse, I tried typing out a few until I heard knocking on a window to my left. Daphne waved at me, beckoning for me to come in.

Oh hell, I hadn't even realized the conference room she'd booked overlooked the front of the City Hall. Likely everyone in that room had seen me texting, then seen Daphne knock on the window to get my attention. Whelp, this was embarrassing.

My cheeks hot, I went in through the glass double doors, heading down the industrial hallway toward the conference room. Hoping for a quick and silent entrance, I opened the door, but sure enough, everyone stopped talking to turn and stare at me. I slipped in, giving Daphne a tight smile. The room was packed. The town's business owners had definitely stepped up, likely bullied by Daphne to take part. I saw

Taylor from Decadent Treats and the owner of the gift shop next door to mine.

And naturally, there was only one open chair. And just as naturally, it was next to Patrick, a sheet of paper with a list sitting in front of it.

The universe was an ass. Why had I tempted it? I shouldn't have even gotten up this morning.

After everyone turned to look at me, Daphne went back to talking about the caterer I'd found, describing the food offerings (salad, chicken, rice, and sweet rolls) while I tried to pull out the chair as quietly as possible. Naturally, the chair got caught on Patrick's and the meeting had to stop again so Patrick could stand up, and I could wrestle my chair out to sit down.

Where was a hole in the floor when you needed it? I focused on Daphne, like her words held the answer to world peace, trying to ignore Patrick to my left. God, he must think I was the biggest idiot, telling him he couldn't sell dolls at his toy store. Was I really that insecure that my store couldn't have any competition? I could outsell him, even with his discount, offering exclusive items he couldn't.

"Kayla." I realized Daphne had likely said my name several times. I'd been staring off into nothing, running my discomfort through my mind for the last few minutes.

"I'm sorry," I said. "What was that?"

Daphne stared at me for a minute, before saying, "I'm going to put you with Issac and Jessica, to coordinate the foster kids' presents. We need to do a count, assign the gifts, and identify any gaps. Then find a way to fill in the gaps—"

"My store will donate whatever is needed," Patrick said.

Of course, his would.

"I'll assist," I said, "With Barbies, baby dolls, whatever. You shouldn't have to be responsible for all of it."

Patrick started to say something, then shrugged, letting it go.

"Okay," Daphne said. "Let's see what we can check off the list. We've got the caterer figured out." She made a dramatic check on the list in front of her and everyone at the table did the same. Fumbling in my purse, I found a pen and made a similar check on my list. "We have the desserts, thanks to Patrick's hard work. And he got them donated, so no expense to us!" Another enthusiastic check. "We've identified who is going to help decorate, and thanks to Patrick, we received donations of artificial trees complete with lights to replace the broken ones we found in storage." Another check. And another shout out to Patrick. Apparently, he'd stepped in and saved the foster kids' dinner, whereas I'd stomped over to his store and thrown a tantrum.

How could I have been so stupid?

"We've got volunteers to figure out the presents, thanks to Kayla, Jessica, and Issac. And we have volunteers to run the event—Kayla, you're helping that night, right?" Daphne asked.

"Of course," I stammered. I'd planned to, at least.

"Perfect," Daphne said with a scribble. "I'm going to assign you to the cookie decorating station, which, again, we got a ton of donations for, thanks to Taylor over at Decadent Treats." She looked down at her checklist with a giant smile. "I think we're going to pull this off. I'm amazed. Thank you all so very much. I'm so happy to see the community committed to making sure these foster kids have a great Christmas." She clapped her hands and everyone in the room joined in, cheering and whooping.

I added a perfunctory and late clap, feeling tired and empty. The foster kids' dinner usually refilled my cup, helping me spread joy for the entire year. But now ... I didn't feel any pride or happiness for the kids. I'd been dealt so many blows, the day didn't even feel real anymore.

Daphne dismissed the room. "Kayla, can you stay? I want to show you where we're going to organize all the presents."

"Of course," I said and then spent the next two minutes fumbling in my bag, ensuring no one would speak to me while the room emptied.

"Did you need me, Patrick?" Daphne asked.

Looking up from where I played with my bag, I glanced over at the door where the tall man hesitated, his green eyes on me. "No, I just thought I'd walk Kayla back to her store."

"Oh, that's okay," I said, trying to force a smile and feeling it turn into a grimace instead. "I might be awhile and you shouldn't leave your store for too long. You've got Mr...." What was the name of that damn robot? "Mr. PlayHand to fix."

Patrick blinked, and Daphne cocked her head to the side. No, damn-it. That wasn't the name. Oh, God—how could today have gotten any worse? I was so embarrassed; nausea swam in my belly. I just wanted to go home and not leave until Christmas was over.

"I don't want to know," Daphne said. "Patrick, thanks for your help, but I am going to go chat with Kayla. You go ... play with Mr. Play ... Oh God, I just can't."

Patrick snickered, which broke the tension, and Daphne cackled. I should laugh too, but I just couldn't. Too much shame today.

"It's—never mind," Patrick said. "Kayla, I'd love to chat with you more if you want to stop by my store later today."

Nope, not going to happen. I was never going to speak to him again. Not because I was angry, but because I was embarrassed. I never should've gone and yelled at him. I shouldn't have come to this meeting.

"Let's go to my office," Daphne said. "Someone probably needs to use this conference room."

"Didn't you need to show me where we were organizing the presents or something?" I asked as I followed her down the hallway and through a few doorways. Daphne cleared a chair of files and an empty Amazon box for me.

"No, that was just an excuse. Coffee?"

"Umm ... sure. You okay?"

She popped a pod in her Keurig and pressed a button. "I'm fine. You're not. What's going on with you? Did something happen between you and Patrick—you could barely look at him."

Groaning, I dropped my head into my hands. "I'm so stupid." I explained how I'd gone off on Patrick for selling dolls in his shop, of all things. "I don't know what's with me," I concluded. "Running over to a business owner and yelling at him isn't like me. Even if he's wrong about how he thinks about toys. He can run his store however he wants."

"Hmmmm ... offering to walk you back to your shop makes me think he's not too angry with you," she handed me the coffee, some cream, and a stirrer. She popped another pod in. "I know Patrick a bit—he's really mellow and impetuous at times. He's a terrible business owner, though he's trying. I don't think he was intentionally competing with you."

I winced. That echoed what Lara had said. "Great. Now I feel even more stupid. It was just a bad choice, and I went and yelled at him for it."

"It would've been a courtesy to tell you he was going to start selling dolls, especially as he hadn't before," she said with a quick laugh. "But just my opinion. You doing okay?" she asked again. "This seems more than just embarrassment."

I shrugged and took a sip of the coffee. It was bitter and

not even remotely warm. Her Keurig must be on its last legs. "It's busy, it's Christmas time and I'm tired." I peeled back the lid of a cream and dumped it into the cup, trying to cut down on the bitterness.

"When's your son coming back for Christmas?" she asked after a pause. "Will he make it for Christmas Eve? You going to close early?"

I dumped in the second cream and took my time stirring it in. "He's not coming back," I said, when I was sure my voice wouldn't crack. "His new job won't let him travel. He called me right before the meeting." I took a sip—the cream hadn't helped.

"Oh, sweetie," Daphne said, putting a hand on my arm. "I'm so sorry. I know how much you were looking forward to having him and his new family come visit. And of course I'm traveling to my parents on Christmas, or I'd invite you to our place, so you wouldn't be all alone."

"It's okay," I said. "I'll have a quiet day. Read a book. Maybe binge watch something before I open the store on the 26th for all the returns and stuff people will buy with their gift cards. It's not like I have any free time right now, so it'll be nice to take some time for me."

"You should invite Patrick and his sister over for Christmas lunch," Daphne said, snapping her fingers. "That would be the perfect apology. Their grandfather just died, and I think they're both a little lost right now. And isn't his sister working for you, anyway?" She grinned gleefully, her eyes alight. "Oh, I love this. It's like a Hallmark movie."

I grimaced. "I'm sure they already have plans."

Someone knocked on her door and a man wearing an obnoxious Christmas sweater stuck their head in. "Mayor Kang is waiting for you in his office," he said. "You're late," he stage-whispered.

"Oh crap," Daphne said. "Let's do coffee tomorrow or the next day and let me know if you have any problems with the presents for the foster kids, but Jessica and Issac are pretty impressive. And we'll do drinks for New Year's Eve, I promise. Maybe get a little drunk as we ring in the New Year."

And with that, she hurried out of her office, trotting down the hall. She trilled apologies to whoever was in the room, and then the office door closed. Setting my disgusting coffee on her desk, I buttoned my coat. I really wanted to go home, open a bottle of wine and pretend today had never happened.

But I couldn't do that to Lara.

## CHAPTER 18

"I can't say how much I appreciate you," I told Lara as we closed the store a few days later. We'd tidied, dusted and restocked the store and were ready for the morning onslaught of customers. I'd prepared all the online orders, and the postman had collected them. The last few days had just flown by in a flurry of customers and orders. This was shaping up to be my best year ever, but things were getting intense. I could no longer guarantee Christmas delivery and had been flooded with requests to see if there was anything I could do. Unfortunately, I wasn't in control of the post office and all I could do was reference their schedule.

I flicked off the lights, leaving just the holiday ones on to cast a twinkling multi-colored glow in my beautiful doll store. Running a toy store was hard, but this was a perfect moment that I tried to embrace. Charles chimed the silver bell on the front door in what I hoped was approval.

"Okay, it's time," Lara said, turning to me. "Before we

both run off. Tell me about your ghost. And I know you're listening," she called into the store's shadows.

"There's not much to tell. Charles came with the building. He's harmless other than his obsession with Mariah Carey." Sure enough, her Christmas song came on. I rolled my eyes as we headed toward the back room where our coats were, but I didn't say anything; we were leaving, and it must get lonely at night. "He communicates through songs, ringing the bell on the door and sometimes messing with decorations. If you focus, sometimes you can feel a breeze as he moves by."

Lara twined her scarf around her neck. "How do you know it's a guy?"

"I don't," I said. "But it feels male to me. And there hasn't been a strong objection to the name. But that's it," I said. "Nothing too crazy—you share the space with a ghost. But not a mean one."

The silver bell on the front door chimed slightly. A small affirmative, I hoped.

"It's kind of cool," Lara said. "Charles is like your theatre ghost. Oh! I know. It's like A Christmas Carol with all the ghosts visiting Scrooge."

I chuckled. "Are you calling me Scrooge?"

"Absolutely not. You're like the opposite of Scrooge. I'm watching too many Christmas movies." She tugged on her lip. "I should find a good horror movie with ghosts."

"Charles was the one who wanted me to open the door to you the Friday after Thanksgiving. Remember? I was closed—but he rang the silver bell so insistently when you knocked that I couldn't ignore it. Which brings me to my next point." I grabbed my purse and passed her an envelope of cash. "Just wanted to say thank you. I couldn't have gotten through these last few weeks without you." Lara looked at me with wide eyes—it was a thick envelope and she glanced inside to see the crisp new $20 bills. "It's not enough," I continued. "And if you're still interested, I'd love your help through the rest of Christmas, but I also want to reimburse you for your time and all the coffees and lunches. I truly don't know what I would've done without you."

"I'm not doing this for money," Lara said, trying to hand back the envelope. "I just love this store. I love the details in the costumes on the collectable dolls and what the porcelain dolls mean to some of the older women who come in. I love talking about the dollhouses and miniatures with those that love them and seeing that ... look on kids' faces. You know. The one that tells you they think their dolls are real, just frozen until they go to bed and then the dolls are going to come to life and ... okay, there's horror movies made because of that feeling."

"I love that look too," I said, ignoring her movie comments. I hated the movies where the dolls came to life and killed everyone, usually starting with the parents. Hell, they'd probably start with me and Lara. I refocused, pushing away the thought. "But you deserve something for all your hard work. And I'm not taking it back."

Lara smiled and tucked the envelope into her purse. "Okay, fine. But lunches are on me until the New Year," she said, before tugging her beanie down over her red hair. "Thank you," she breathed. "It means a lot. And I appreciate you giving me something to do for the time being. It's been helping a lot to get through these last few weeks. Gramps accumulated a ton of random stuff, and Patrick and I can't figure out what to do with all of it. Don't stay too long," she called out before swinging open the front door and stepping out into the Christmas card-like street, glittering with snow,

Christmas decorations sparkling in the light from the streetlights.

As I'd done every evening since my horrible behavior with Patrick, I took a minute to walk through my store, appreciating the work I'd put into it, taking the moment for gratitude for the busy days, for the ability to do what I wanted to do. I reflected on all I'd done over the years. With blood, sweat, and tears, I'd been able to make a living owning a doll store and giving imagination, safety, and love to children—all the things dolls provided. Owning this store helped to fill in the gaps in my heart from being a foster kid and not having anyone care enough about me to allow me to have any toys. This was an important ritual I needed to help me get back into the Christmas spirit.

It was kind-of working, but deep in my heart, I just wanted Christmas to be over.

I ordered a pizza for takeout, and climbed into my car, stopping only to collect the cardboard box and heading toward my little house, the smell of garlic, melted cheese, and tomato sauce making my mouth water. I was five minutes to home, thinking about the large glass of red wine I'd enjoy with my pizza when I passed by Patrick's store. The beautiful windows holding nothing but wire racks were dark —but I could see the glow of a light coming from the back of the store. Someone was working late.

I pulled off to the side of the road at a stop sign and texted Lara.

> There's a light on in your brother's store. Is he being robbed, or is he still working? It's almost eight.

She responded almost immediately.

> Probably working late. He's stressed. He got an estimate to fix that damn robot and it's not going to be cheap. Running a toy store is harder than he thought it'd be.

Of course it was—the margins were tight, and over-ordering one wrong shipment that didn't sell might mean you were eating beans and boxed pasta for a month, unable to pay yourself. And then there were the unseen costs. Insurance for slip and falls, online store fees, décor for the holidays, the list went on and on of the little things that made this life so much harder. Parents screaming at you because you sold the last Barbie, a child throwing up on the merchandise, someone sneaking a dog in that peed on a miniature room display (true story!).

I looked at the pizza box next to me. Running a toy store was hard. I knew that. I lost inventory every month in broken doll house furniture and stolen toys. It was hard to find the balance between helping children, helping their parents and turning a profit. I'd almost closed three times, giving it all up, and looking into getting a corporate job.

Maybe I could pay him back for yelling at him by offering a little advice. Maybe he just needed someone to help. Someone that knew what they were doing. Someone who knew about toys.

I turned around and pulled into a parking spot in front of his store. Grabbing the pizza, I knocked on the front door.

## CHAPTER 19

*I* was shivering by the time Patrick came to the door, the pizza box in my hand steaming in the icy air.

"Kayla? What's wrong? Did you get into a car accident? Are you okay?"

He stood aside and let me into his darkened toy store. In my store, when the lights were out, the doll's display cases and dollhouses on display with tiny lamps in the windows created either a whimsical or a creepy feeling, depending on your mood. But in his store, the boxes of toys on the shelves just looked like stacked boxes in the dark. The robot arm was a dark shadow in the middle of the floor. The store smelled of dust with an undercurrent of WD-40. There was no magic, no creativity. Patrick's store lacked imagination—maybe that was the problem.

"I saw your light on as I drove by. And Lara said you're stressed, and I had a pizza and it's Christmas time..." Nerves swam in my stomach. I shouldn't have come. This was even more ridiculous than coming over to his store a few days ago to yell at him. I looked down at the scuffed floor. "Toy stores are hard to make a living at," I continued with a shrug, trying not to sound weird. "I don't know. Maybe you need someone who knows something about toy stores to talk to."

He pushed his glasses up his nose, silent for a few beats too long. He was still good looking, with those full lips and high cheekbones, but his sexy morning beard had turned into unkept scruff, and bags under his eyes pulled his face down. This place must be killing him.

"I'll go," I said. "You were probably just heading out." For all I knew, he had a date. A ping of envy sparked in my chest. Where had that come from? I wasn't interested in him in that way, right? I just felt bad for the guy.

"I was definitely not expecting to see you here tonight," Patrick said. "After you came by to yell at me, I figured you wouldn't want to talk to me ever again."

"I know. I shouldn't have done that. I've had too much Christmas."

He chuckled at the refrain from parents and teachers to explain kids' bad behavior at this time of year.

"Or we could just have pizza and talk about TV shows or Christmas or life," I said. "I mean, my son's not coming home or anything for Christmas day, so there's that. His new job won't let him travel, or they won't let him have the time off." I was growing warm in the store, my babbling heating my cheeks. Hell. He must think I'm insane.

Patrick leaned back his head and laughed. "You and my sister are so much alike. Come on back. I have napkins and I'm starving."

I followed him down a shadowy aisle toward the light coming from the storage room. "How old is your son?" he asked over his shoulder.

"Twenty-two. He just moved to Arizona for a job that's perfect for him and his new family."

"You don't look like you would have a twenty-two-year-old."

I'd heard variations on this before and forced a laugh. That was never the compliment people thought it was. "Thanks," I said. "I was eighteen when I had him. Nothing more than a teenager myself."

I saw him doing the math in his head, calculating my age, and comparing it to what he knew about me. But luckily, he didn't ask about Luke's dad, or make any more comments about my supposed youth. He just led me into his storage room, and I followed him between wire racks stacked high with boxes of toys, basically the same look he had in his store. Hell—he could restock his store by rolling out wire carts. I resisted shaking my head as I followed him to a desk similar to mine, stacked with papers that almost buried his computer screen. An inventory program lit up the monitor. Ah yes—the fun count of trying to figure out how much more to order so you had enough in stock, but not so much, the toys just took up room in the storage area or had to be returned. Patrick opened a desk drawer and riffled through to find napkins and a few beat-up plates.

I set the pizza box on a pile of papers and flipped the top. Inside was gooey melted cheese topped with pineapple and ham. I reached for a slice, my stomach growling.

"Hang on," Patrick said. "I had a customer give me a bottle of wine because I helped her carry a giant box to her car. Luckily, it's not an expensive wine, and it has a screw top, because I don't have a corkscrew lying around. Honestly, I think the only reason she gave me the wine was so she could suggest we share it together."

I raised an eyebrow. "That's an interesting way to get dates."

"A little too weird for me," he said. "But she insisted I keep the wine, even after I said no thanks." He pulled out two mugs emblazoned with the store's name, and, twisting the top, poured the red wine in. "Sorry, I don't have wine glasses." He passed a mug to me.

"Considering I randomly stopped by with pizza and you randomly had wine, I'm fine drinking out of the mugs. Cheers," I said, clinking my glass to his. I took a sip. It was a typical red wine, but would balance the pizza well. "I didn't even ask if you like Hawaiian pizza," I said, taking a slice and biting in. The pizza was cool, but still good, the flavors of tomato sauce marrying well with the melted mozzarella.

"All pizza is good," he said, grabbing his own slice. "I forgot to eat dinner and at this point, I'd eat anything."

We were quiet, other than the chewing, sipping, and wiping our fingers on the paper napkins until we could eat without gulping. Patrick leaned back with a groan. "I was so hungry. And Lara and I haven't done the weekly shopping. We've been living on pasta and cans of soup. This was perfect. Thank you."

I snagged another piece of pizza. "So what's going on?" I asked Patrick. "Why are you working so late?"

"It's the holidays," he said with a shrug.

I nodded and took a bite, waiting for him to say more. When he didn't, I said, "And that's a hard time of year for us toy store owners. It's the busiest from Thanksgiving to mid-January."

"It is."

I gave it a few minutes for him to fill in the silence. When I couldn't stand it anymore, I spoke. "But it's also our most profitable. And the most fun too," I said. "It's Christmas! The one time of year when all the Christmas spirit comes out. And people are willing to do just a bit more for others."

"All the requirements. The have-tos, or someone's Christmas is ruined," Patrick countered.

I nodded slowly. "That can be true if people aren't flexible. But I love watching the kids buying for siblings, vacillating between different choices and trying to do the math on the money they have versus how much it costs. And then they come up and buy the present themselves, with their parents standing by ready to help, just in case. It's so cute. And I love it when they come into the store and make lists for Santa, believing, like truly believing, he comes down the chimney and leaves presents for them under the tree."

"But the parents are terrible. They think their kids' Christmas is ruined if there's not enough presents—never mind the debt or the expectations to have more and more under the tree each year. And Christmas just keeps getting bigger. It's not enough to offer free gift wrapping—it has to be fancy gift wrapping. And god-forbid you charge for it to cover your expenses. That's not in the Christmas spirit," Patrick said, pushing his glasses up his nose.

I snickered. "Sounds like you're running a toy store at Christmas. It's easy to get burnt out. That's why I try to focus on the kids and doing good for others. That's part of the reason I have the Giving Tree in my store and help with the foster kids' dinner."

Patrick sighed. "I'll be honest; never really thought about the kids buying presents for each other. I just try to steer them and their parents toward something in the store Answer their questions, that type of thing. Try not to let them leave or order online from a big box store. I've never thought about it like you do." He looked down at the pile of papers on his desk—printouts of inventory sheets, bills and the like. There were a few yellow envelopes, warnings of overdue bills.

"Can I ask?" I started. "Why did you open this store? Especially if you don't love toys?"

He tossed his half-eaten slice of pizza back onto the paper plate and took a big sip of wine from the mug. "It was my grandfather's idea."

## CHAPTER 20

"The one that died?" I asked.
"Lara told you?"
"Not much. Just that he died, and she was in town to help go through his things, help you adjust. I'm sorry he died," I murmured. I didn't add, especially at Christmas. Patrick might be a little Christmased out right now.

He topped off his mug and poured more wine into mine.

"The toy store was my grandfather's idea. That's why I leased this place and bought the inventory cheaply from another store that went out of business. He always wanted to work in a toy store, play with the kids, talk about toys with them. He had these grand plans to build toy train tracks all over the store, so the kids could watch the trains go around the tracks."

Kids adored watching model trains go between various buildings and tunnels. Many toy stores used that as a theme to bring families in. I wondered why Patrick had never done it.

"Honestly, he wanted to contrast with your store. Yours

was dolls. This one was going to be a little more boy focused."

"You opened two years ago," I said. "He got his wish."

Patrick took a big drink of wine. "Kind-of. He had a stroke a week from opening."

Oh. Well, that sounded dreadful.

"And he got to see it open and would come sometimes and sit in here…" He gulped down his wine.

"But he didn't get to build the train tracks or create the store he dreamed of," I breathed.

Patrick shook his head. "And I'm not really into trains, not like he is—was. And I'd planned on redecorating, but—anyway, I'm hoping Mr. ToyDrop will help. I want to build something more than just a store. Kind-of like yours."

I nodded. It wasn't a bad idea. He just didn't know how to do it properly. Mr. ToyDrop was not the answer. But I wasn't sure it was my place to tell him that. I took a sip of wine instead.

"Can I ask you a question?" He leaned forward, his elbows on his knees.

"Always."

"Lara says your store is very busy. That you have many online orders and people travel for hundreds of miles—part of their family Christmas traditions—to come to your store. And you had that write up in the New York Times. But are you actually turning a profit? After you pay rent, and supplies and yourself and electrical and all that?"

I actually did. My bills were paid, I could reinvest profits into my store and still pay myself a good salary. But telling him that wouldn't help. It wasn't about the money. I loved what I did and built a career because of that. Money, though important because I needed to eat and pay Franklin and

Lara, was secondary to me. Creating a life I was proud of was more important.

"Do you like toys?" I asked. "Like truly. I mean, you've said we're on opposite sides of the toy debate. You think they're disposable and I disagree. And my store speaks to that. To me, toys aren't disposable; they're precious."

"I like toys," he said. "I truly do, or I wouldn't have opened the toy store just for Gramps. Just think kids don't really care about them; not anymore. I mean, look at all the unboxing videos. They just care about the potential of what's inside. Not the actual toy. That's why kids love unwrapping presents on Christmas morning so much. It's not about what they actually get—it's about seeing what's inside. I don't know. Things have changed since Gramps was a kid. Heck, since we were kids. They don't seem to love toys as much as they used to."

I nodded. I knew what he was talking about—the unboxing YouTube videos had affected the toy industry, spawning the sale of blind boxes and toys that were nothing more than look-what's-inside, rather than actual toys. "I don't sell that stuff," I said. "Because I want my shoppers to WANT their toys; to love or have a use for them. I have this one brand of doll—sells well online and I have a therapist who buys them—for adults. They're dolls that can be customized and used to heal trauma. People use the dolls to have imaginary "discussions" with those people. They're too scared to have the conversations in real life, or the person is dead. Some even destroy the dolls. This one woman sent me a video of her running over a doll, then backing up and doing it again, before setting it on fire." I shrugged. "She mailed me what was left of it, asking me to bury it for her."

"That's a bit out there." Patrick frowned. "Though I guess

it's not much different from people throwing darts at a picture of someone's face."

I shrugged. "She said it helped her. Helped her come to terms with her trauma."

"Did you bury it?"

"Of course. There's power in that."

Patrick topped off my mug and poured the rest of the wine into his. "So you're basically selling voodoo dolls?"

I laughed. "No. But—okay, I guess kind of. Except for the part about it causing harm to the person it's representing." I took a sip of wine, the jammy flavor hitting my tongue. "I hope it's not causing harm, at least. Though there would be a market for that."

He chuckled. "Other than the trauma dolls, you sell things for kids to fall in love with?"

"Mostly. I also sell miniatures for making rooms or dollhouses. Adults love them. There's an enormous market online—most big cities have a miniature or dollhouse museum."

"Wait, what?" he turned to his computer, fingers flying across the keyboard. "I have to check—no way—there totally is. I got into the wrong market. No one falls in love with Legos and Nerf guns."

"But they do," I said. "You ever seen a kid build a Millennium Falcon? Then play with Luke and Han, pretending they're fighting Darth Vader? That's love. Or walking around with a Nerf gun in their pocket, pretending to defend their family from an alien invasion? That's love."

"Not to all."

"No, not to all," I said. "And I know some of the kids purchasing the outfits for the Fashion Dream Dolls just want the hunt for the exclusives. They'll brag about it to their friends, make their friends jealous, and then forget about it. I'm not that blind."

"See, disposable," he said. Patrick was getting a little buzzed, starting to slur a bit.

"But not to all," I conceded. "And maybe that love is transitory, but it's still real." Like my relationship with Luke's father. Maybe there were parallels I didn't want to think about. "Didn't you ever love a stuffed animal?" I asked.

He leaned back and thought. "I think there was one. It was this koala bear I named Ratty."

"Ratty?"

"Yeah, I think it was after a character on a TV show." He leaned forward, thinking. "But I couldn't sleep without that thing. And I remember my mom tucking him next to me when I was home sick from school."

"And did it make you feel better?" I asked.

Patrick started to shake his head, then stopped. "He did. I'd forgotten. God, I loved that koala." He finished the wine in his mug. "I remember getting into the car ... I haven't thought about this in years ... but I didn't have him and made my mom go in and get him. I thought something ... bad ... I don't know ... can't describe it."

"You just had to have him," I filled in, enjoying the light of memory in Patrick's eyes. My heart gave a thump of appreciation. "Your koala protected you, and you protected him. And that's what I try to give at my store. Not just dolls, but an entire experience. The imagination, the whimsy, the love."

He nodded slowly. "Okay. I'm kind-of getting it."

"And people will pay a bit more for the experience. And it doesn't take much. Just add some displays. Let the kids touch the toys. You're on the right track with Mr. PlayHand—I mean..."

He laughed, a huge guffaw. "Okay, Mr. ToyDrop is a terrible name. I get it."

I took a bit gulp of wine, finishing my glass before saying, "If I may ... your store shouldn't look like a storage room."

He groaned. "Yeah, I know. That was a mistake. I was trying to make it easier for parents just to find what they needed and grab it and go. I figured my store would be for the busy parents or the impulse purchasers." He rubbed the back of his neck. "But I see your point. I don't know ... might be too late. I'm pretty deep in the hole."

"Oh, come on," I said, the wine talking for me. "The Fashion Dream Dolls must be selling well." There wasn't much sarcasm there—nope, not from me!

He snorted. "They are. And I have so many of them—got a great deal. But you're right, I should've said something to you before I started selling them. I should just sell them to you for what I paid."

"Now you're being a poor salesman," I said. "You should offer them to me for what you paid for them and 10% more. But you can sell whatever you want; I shouldn't have gotten so upset."

We smiled at each other, and I suddenly felt much lighter, much more at peace. And liking this rival toy store owner a lot more than I had. A glance at my phone told me it was after ten. "I should let you get some sleep," I said, standing up. "Let me know if you want some help with anything here. You're going to have to find your thing, but this store could be really amazing."

Patrick walked me out between the dark aisles and gave me that side-ways grin. "Long as I don't sell dolls. There's no point," he said before I could protest. "You have the market cornered on those. Thank you for the pizza and the talk.

## WRAPPING PAPER RIVALS

"Ichabod is doing good, by the way," he said. "I've managed to keep that damn cat inside for a bunch of days now."

"Well, that's good." I missed Ichabod more than I thought I would, but was happy he had a home and wouldn't freeze to death in the snow.

He unlocked the door for me, and I stepped outside. It was cold, but the sky was clear, the stars sparkling. My breath puffed out into the night air.

"If you ever want to come and visit him, just text. Lara knows the way."

"I will," I said. "And let me know if you want to talk more about your toy store." God, now I was repeating myself. "Owning one is hard."

"It is," he confirmed, looking down at the ground.

He looked so sad I impulsively gave him a quick hug. "It'll be okay," I said. "You'll get through this."

He clung, his arms wrapped around me, a combination of gratitude and also need. He pressed his chin into my head, heaving a deep breath. When I pulled back, there were tears in his eyes.

"I'm sorry," he said. "It's been a terrible few months."

The snow floated between us, coating our shoulders, getting caught on our eyelashes. "I'm so sorry your grandfather's dream isn't how he wanted it," I said. "He must have been an amazing man." I'd sensed Lara's loss too, in her need for something to do, and that sense of being lost.

"He was. He'd tell me not to worry so much," he snickered. "Money comes and goes—that's normal. Anyway, sorry to break down on you. Thanks for the pizza and the talk."

"Anytime," I said. And meant it.

He leaned over and kissed my cheek, and somehow, I turned my head, so our lips brushed. The kiss deepened, sweet but enough to send a zing through my body to coil in my belly.

God, what was I doing?

"Merry Christmas," I said, pulling away and feeling foolish. I got into my car. Patrick stood on the snowy sidewalk in front of his store and watched me drive away.

Merry Christmas? What kind of response was that? And why had I kissed him? Must have been the wine and all the Christmasness.

I was really starting to hate this season. It made us do stupid things.

# CHAPTER 21

I lay awake that night, staring up at my bedroom's ceiling despite the exhaustion thrumming through my veins. The peacefulness of my bedroom wasn't working tonight. I desperately needed sleep; it was the weekend before Christmas and all the last-minute shoppers would flood Old Towne looking for the perfect waited-too-long-gifts. And on top of that, I was going to meet Issac and Jessica at two tomorrow to complete the donations for the foster kids to make sure there weren't any gaps, and each foster child had a present. And everything still had to get wrapped and tagged. I was fast at gift wrapping because of my store, but wrapping presents for eighty-plus children would still take hours.

It was going to be an insane few days. But all I could think about was Patrick. I'd misjudged him. He'd made massive mistakes opening his toy store and it would be hard to keep it open, but he hadn't done it to make money; he'd done it for the love of a grandfather who hadn't even gotten to enjoy it. And that kiss! It had been so fast, and so sweet, but I couldn't stop thinking about it. Why had I kissed him? Why had I even stopped by his store? I wasn't a spur-of-the-moment kind of gal.

And why had I kissed him? Did I like him? I mean, I kind-of did after hearing about his koala and grandfather ... but ... dating was out of the question. Right?

Right!

Finally, at two a.m. I gave up and made coffee. Sleep wasn't going to happen. Grabbing a granola bar, I logged onto my store's website. Online orders had slowed to a trickle, comparatively, but were still coming in. Weird. Oh, wait ... most of the orders were for the same doll, a Bratz doll that was the popular ... aha. Logging onto big box retailers' sites, I realized those stores had run out and weren't able to ship until ... February? That was nuts. I still had sixteen of those dolls, and while I couldn't guarantee Christmas, I could guarantee New Year's Eve. I fell into the routine of checking inventory and eventually, pouring my coffee into a to-go cup, drove to the store. It was four a.m., the snow glistening in the street lamps, peaceful before the insanity of Christmas shopping began.

I opened the backdoor, my eyes falling on the little cat bed I'd bought for Ma—Ichabod. I really should give that to Patrick. It did no good here. But then I'd have to see him, talk to him ... and yeah ... nope. I was just going to ignore him until the insanity of Christmas was over and I came back to my senses.

I began to wrap online orders, boxing, labeling and getting them ready for the post office to pick up. The mindless activity was soothing and my worries about the kiss with Patrick took a step back. When I was done with the online orders, I started cleaning the storage room, refusing to think about anything other than what was in front of me, until the back door swung open again.

I startled. "Morning!" Lara called. "I thought I might beat you here, but I saw your car—oh my God." She looked around at the spotless storage room. "How long have you been here?"

Good god, what time was it? I checked my phone. It was 8:30 am. We were opening at nine all this week. I'd spent the last four hours wrapping and cleaning? How had that happened? I'd never lost time like that before. I stretched out my cramped back—I was going to need some ibuprofen and a vat of coffee.

"I couldn't sleep," was what I meant to say, but instead, said, "I kissed your brother."

"Ohhhhhhh..." Lara leaned a hip on a shelf. "When? Where? How? I don't think you spent the night at Gramp's."

"What? No! God no."

"Ah," she said. "It was a terrible kiss, wasn't it? That seems so weird. He had so many girlfriends in high school and college. I remember walking in on him making out on the couch with one of them."

"Oh, shut up," I said, exhaustion loosening my filter. "We open in thirty minutes. We've gotta get set up."

"It was a great kiss, wasn't it?" She followed me over to the counter as I flicked on the store lights and tried to ignore her.

"Play instrumental Christmas music," I instructed the sound system and spritzed a bit of cypress scent into the air.

Mariah Carey came on.

"Oh, come on Charles," I snapped. "I can't take this right now!" The silver bell on the door chimed, but I couldn't tell if it was approval or negotiation as Mariah Carey continued to play. "We need to focus. Let's get open."

"And then you tell me all about the kiss."

With a groan, I told Lara how I'd gone to Patrick's shop last night on a whim with a pizza and how he and I had chatted about the toy store. And their grandfather. "Sounds like your Gramps had some cool ideas for the toy store."

"He did," Lara confirmed, grabbing the stepladder and duster to take a sweep at some of the stock on the upper shelves. "But I think when Gramps had his stroke, Patrick kind-of lost interest. And then he couldn't afford everything he wanted to do." Her voice floated up over the aisles. "He bought some stock he had problems selling and then had an insurance claim for a slip and fall and then had a bunch of boxes, 'go missing' because his inventory system was so bad. I think one of the kids who worked for him stole them, but he couldn't prove anything. And now he's just kind-of stuck making enough money to survive, but not enough to invest in the business."

I nodded, counting the cash in the register and making a note. "I know the feeling. I couldn't draw a salary for the first year and the next year I kept having to funnel what I could back into the business."

"He'll figure it out," she said. "But tell me more about this kiss!"

I glanced toward the front door where I could see people waiting in their cars for us to open and sighed. I couldn't believe I was going to share this. I'd never been great at the girl talk so many in high school and college had naturally done. "He walked me out. And ... he told me thank you. I don't know what happened," I said. "But I gave him a hug and then he kissed my cheek and then I turned my head—"

"And you were kissing," she said. "I love it. You two are perfect for each other. Two toy store owners in the same town. So now what? Are you going to meet for coffee? I think he actually likes you."

"Oh please. Maybe he was just kissing back to be polite and then washed his mouth out with mouthwash afterwards. Maybe I kissed him, and it was without his permission. Maybe he thinks I harassed him. Or maybe—"

Lara's laugh stopped my sleep-deprived babbling. She climbed down the ladder and tucked the duster and ladder away. "He hasn't dated anyone in a while. And I doubt he thought you harassed him or anything. If my brother didn't want to be kissed by you, he would've stopped it."

"He doesn't know me. I could be a serial harasser." I folded my arms against my chest.

"But you're not. And if he thought you were, he wouldn't have asked me this morning to find out if you had plans for Christmas dinner. I think he wants to invite you over and now that I know you guys kissed—it's just perfect." She clapped her hands. "This is like a Christmas movie!"

"You've been watching too much of the Hallmark Channel," I said.

"Guilty," she sang out as she sashayed down an aisle checking everything to make sure we were ready to open.

I straightened out the counter, thinking. Christmas dinner? He was inviting me to Christmas dinner? Or Lara was. Or was it, Patrick? Or both of them? God, this was confusing! I should've never gone over to his shop last night, never should've hugged him and definitely shouldn't have kissed him!

Lara's voice traveled through the store. "I mean, you don't have plans, right? Your son and his family aren't coming still?"

"No, they're not," I said. "I just—"

"Think about it," Lara said softly, coming back up to the

front. "I know I'm teasing you, but no pressure. My brother is one of the most chill people out there. He wouldn't want you to obsess about a little kiss. And if you don't want to ... do anything with him." A flush touched her pale cheeks, and I giggled. Despite all her teasing, she was embarrassed. "He's my brother," she said with a chuckle of her own. "I don't like to think of him dating. It's gross. But he's a nice guy. You could do worse. Just think about Christmas dinner. But not a big deal if you can't make it."

"Let's get the store opened," I said, going to the front door and unlocking it, waving at the customers staying warm in their cars. Doors started opening as adults and their kids climbed out, their breath puffing in the cold air. "And I'm going to need more coffee. My treat. I'll go across the street. You're in charge of the store."

"Aye, aye, Captain," Lara said with a salute and a wink.

## CHAPTER 22

*A*round two that afternoon, I left Lara in charge and drove toward City Hall, my trunk full of donations from the Giving Tree. My store alone had collected twenty-six donations for the kids; I couldn't believe it! I loved how this community came through, even when things might be tight. Though my body hummed with exhaustion and sleep deprivation, I felt amazing. The foster kids' dinner was going to be an incredible night—one that would boost these kids when they needed it the most. I hummed along with Rockin' Around the Christmas Tree, my mood lighter than it had been since Luke had told me he wasn't going to make it to Christmas this year.

I passed by a man walking down the street wearing a flannel and my mind immediately turned to Patrick. Why had we kissed? Why could I not stop thinking about his green eyes and the way the muscles in his back had felt when I'd hugged him? He'd felt so good to hug—I hadn't hugged anyone, other than Luke or occasionally Daphne, in years.

Maybe it had just been too long between relationships.

But relationships were so messy and so much work. I wasn't interested in beginning one.

Right?

And Patrick thought toys were disposable, which went against who I was and what I thought about toys and children. And yet he hadn't gotten into the toy business for the love of children or toys. He'd built Toys and Games for his grandfather, not for himself, fulfilling a dream that wasn't his. There was loyalty and love in that. Sweetness and caring. And his grandfather hadn't even been able to truly enjoy it. Now the toy store was a duty, a memorial. A legacy that hadn't been well thought out. Maybe it kind of made a weird sense that he thought of toys as disposable.

It might be fun to date another toy store owner. Someone that knew what it was like to deal with the toy distributors and go to the toy conferences with. I bet he'd never been to one. Someone who knew how frustrating the meltdowns in the middle of the store were because parents wouldn't buy a certain toy. Or the desire not to judge the parent whose child had everything and was still demanding more. Someone who knew the frustration the week after Christmas with all the returns, and the number of times I'd have to say, "I'm sorry—we can't accept a toy that's been played with." Someone that would know what I meant when I spotted a parent with haunted eyes returning toys because something bad had happened, and they wouldn't be able to afford new tires or a new washing machine if the gifts their child had received didn't get exchanged for money.

But did Patrick even see those things? Or were they just part of the business for him?

And did I want to find out?

I pulled into the parking garage next to City Hall and got out of my car to pop open the trunk. Twenty-six different toys were a lot, even though I'd put as many as I could into shopping bags. I was going to have to make multiple trips to get them all inside. I loaded up my arms, stacking the toys as high as they would go, without the risk of dropping them, my feet crunching on the salt someone had spread through the garage.

"Here, let me help," said a familiar voice, reaching around to grab for the top toys on the stack.

Oh God. I knew that voice. "Hi there," I said, turning. The cool air had added color to his cheeks and his green eyes nearly matched the green beanie he wore. He was so gorgeous in this moment. My eyes went to his lips. I was tempted to drop all the presents and dive into his arms.

"Hi," he said, staring down at me, the toys clutched between us.

Okay, now what?

A four-door sped toward us, pulling into an adjacent spot. Grateful for the distraction, I turned to see who the driver was. "Hey you two," Daphne said with a wave as she got out of her Prius. "I'm so glad I caught you. Are those the donations? Let me help."

With our arms full of toys, we went inside City Hall to the conference room designated for the presents. Issac and Jessica were already there, lists in hand, sorting and putting sticky notes with the children's names on the gifts assigned to them.

"Oh, thank goodness," Jessica said as we put our piles down. "I was starting to panic. Need help grabbing the rest?"

"The rest?" I asked. "This is all—twenty-six gifts. This is the most donations I've ever gotten."

Issac and Jessica exchanged looks.

"What's wrong?" Daphne asked.

"We're short about thirty presents," Jessica said, flipping her braided hair over her shoulder.

"Even with these?" I asked.

"Even with these," she confirmed. "I mean, you can still make up the difference right," she said, turning to Patrick.

"Ummm," he said. "I mean, we're short thirty presents? That's a lot to..."

"Uh, no we're not," Daphne said. "That was the one thing we had figured out. Jeffrey promised before his surgery. He said we were going to get enough donations, easy-peasy. And I quote."

Jessica and Issac shrugged as one.

"Do you have the list?" Daphne collected it. "This is the one that says who's getting which gifts. What about the one that says which businesses are collecting donations?"

Again, Jessica and Issac shrugged.

"Let me go check some emails." Daphne strode from the room.

"We'll get started here organizing the gifts," Patrick said.

"We'll figure out what we're missing," I said.

We spent the next hour sorting and labeling the presents we had, making note of the ones we didn't have. Patrick worked hard, but didn't speak other than to move the toys around or confirm pairings of children with their toys. But his brow was scrunched, worry pulling his lips down.

Maybe he regretted that kiss after all. Maybe I'd totally misread everything, made up a story about him because I felt bad for him. Maybe he really was the jerk I'd thought he was.

Daphne came back into the conference room. "Okay," she said with a gigantic sigh. "I've dug through everything. I'm thinking that Jeffrey never asked for donations. The ones we've gotten are from businesses who are used to donating and didn't need to be asked." She licked her lips. "So the dinner is tomorrow night. And we're short about thirty presents."

"Twenty-eight," Jessica said from where she knelt on the floor. She passed her sheet of paper up to Issac, who leaned back and stretched out his back. "Some of the requests are very specific, things like Luke Skywalker's X-Wing Lego and that robot T-Rex that is sold out online. We do have most of the girl-specific ones though, probably because your shoppers donated so much." Jessica nodded at me.

"There are few requests for more of the Fashion Dream Dolls," I said. "And two specific Barbies? The holiday one for this year and the pizza maker one, right?"

Issac nodded.

"I've got those in stock," I said. "And I'll wrap them at my store and bring them over to save us time." I pulled out my phone and checked shipping from the big box stores. "Anything we order online isn't guaranteed by tomorrow. Even if we pay for expedited shipping. And we can't give out pictures of presents or order confirmations."

"Absolutely not," Daphne said.

"I've got most of this." Patrick leaned over me to read the list. "I can make up a lot of the difference." My heart went out to him. If he was struggling for money, donating fifteen or so gifts were going to cut into his bottom-line. I knew how much every penny counted.

"Okay," Daphne said. "Whatever is left after Patrick's donations, Jessica and Issac do you mind driving into Bisham to pick up? But money is super tight, so don't go crazy."

The two college interns nodded, and we finished stacking the toys, Patrick and I walking out together.

"That's so nice of you to donate the toys," I started. "I know ... fifteen toys is a lot to donate."

He shrugged. "It's okay. I'm starting to see the value of toys. And everyone, especially foster kids, need to have a good Christmas."

Maybe that kiss hadn't been such a bad idea after all.

"Foster kids have it really rough," he said. "I know some of them are foster kids because bad things happen, and the court takes them away from their parents. But did you know some of these kids are actually given up by their parents?"

My heart chilled. "Sometimes parents don't have a choice."

He made a face, pushing his glasses up his nose. "There's always a choice. There's lots of help for parents struggling. Food stamps, assistance programs for daycare, Boys and Girls Club. Family. Friends."

"Some people don't have that," I stated, my voice flat.

"They just have to look for it. I mean, I get having kids isn't easy, but these are THEIR kids! Make an effort. Don't just give your kids up because things get rough!"

This was so much worse than thinking toys were disposable. This was my life. My mother loved me; she had no choice when she'd put me in the foster program. It was that or starve. I'd had my therapy and forgiven her. She'd made the best choice she could've made at the time.

And I'd never get to ask her if she would've made a different one.

Tears filled my eyes as her loss and the way I'd grown up hit me like a sledgehammer. My breath caught and the sound of my heartbeat filled my ears. Holy hell, I was having an anxiety attack.

"Kayla? What's wrong?" Patrick touched my elbow. I swiped at the tears running down my cheeks while I fought for control. "Kayla, talk to me."

2. 3. 4. 5. And out. 1. 2. 3. 4. 5. And in.

I breathed and counted, ignoring Patrick, who likely realized I was fighting for control. "You okay?" he asked after a few breath cycles. "What happened?"

The tears still ran, but my heart didn't feel like it would explode from my chest. I looked up at him, into those beautiful green eyes I'd been starting to relish looking into, and said, "I was a foster kid. My mom gave me up because she had no choice."

I ripped my arm away and strode away, my tears cold on my face. Now I knew. We'd never work. Best to find out now before I invested a lot of time in him.

Before he really hurt me.

## CHAPTER 23

"*Y*ou ready?" Lara said the next night as we stood outside the city's convention hall, ready to go into the foster kids' dinner. I tugged on my skirt, smoothing out a wrinkle. I didn't care what Patrick thought of me, and yet I'd chosen my outfit for tonight with care, taking a few minutes to dress up my normal hair style and apply more make-up.

"You look beautiful," Lara told me. "I love that dress." I hadn't had a chance to buy a true holiday dress this year and wore a sweeping navy dress with tiny sparkles in it; definitely dressier than the jeans and sweater I normally wore to the store. While the foster kids' dinner wasn't a formal event, I liked to dress up for it, do my part to make it seem a bit more special.

"Thank you," I said. "So do you."

Lara had gone for the more traditional Christmas theme wearing a plaid skirt and green sweater paired with black boots and a green beret atop her curly red hair. She looked like a Christmas doll.

"Thank you," she said. "I'm so excited to see the kids get their presents."

"Me too." We almost didn't make it. Issac and Jessica had to search multiple stores for some of the more popular toys that Patrick and I hadn't had. They'd finally found the last one over fifty miles away this afternoon and had raced to get back in time for it to be wrapped and placed beneath the tree with the rest.

Lara flung open the doors, a dramatic gesture, though one door stuck half-way open. The dinner hadn't started yet, but things were almost ready. Playful Christmas music was on the speakers and there were multiple trees, all different sizes, their lights twinkling, decorated with glittering ornaments. Someone had wrapped garland, tinsel, and tiny twinkling lights on every surface they possibly could, creating a fun, if a bit tacky, environment. But the kids would love it, and that was what mattered. I waved to the Santa who'd volunteered to take pictures with the kids, where he stood munching a cookie, his beard around his chin, and went to the cookie decorating station where I'd spend most of my evening. Grabbing boxes from under the table, I set up everything I might need: plates, cookies, icing, candied decorations, and most importantly, wet-wipes for everyone's hands once they'd finished decorating. I also set up a little area with paper cookies the kids could draw on. The gesture was nice, but I doubted any of the kids would participate—not when they could decorate and eat a real cookie.

Daphne swept over, wearing a pretty dress of sparkling red, and handed me a tacky apron with a Santa embroidered on it. "Can't let that outfit get ruined," she said, and I gratefully tied it over my clothes. "Thank you for your help. We wouldn't have gotten this done without yours and Patrick's help."

"Happy to do it," I said, deciding I didn't like how I'd organized the sprinkles and moving things around on the table.

"I promise, next year will be better. I won't put Jeffrey in charge, for starters."

I smiled. "Turned out okay in the end. And this looks amazing! The kids are going to love it."

Jessica called out to the room, "everyone ready?" and swung open the doors. Kids and their host parents came in, the younger ones running in and exclaiming over the decorations and the number of presents under the trees. The teenagers slouched in, their faces in their phones, congregating at the soda and snack stations. I made a mental note to give them something else to do next year. Maybe a trivia game or something. Teenage foster kids had it the hardest of any and often struggled at events like this because they were catered to the younger ones. But a few wandered over to my table, quickly making cookies they took back to their corners to munch on. Foster parents cycled through, and I analyzed body language, trying to find out if these parents actually cared—even if it was just a little—for the children under their care. I always struggled a bit tonight, trying not to let my own memories of being a foster kid and how I was treated at Christmas time overshadow the night.

I knew the agencies were doing a better job of vetting foster parents now and hoped these kids didn't go through the neglect and horrors I and so many others had. Feeling still a little raw from Patrick's comment, I breathed in and out a few times, pushing the memories and emotions aside. Tonight wasn't about me.

Several of the children approached my station. I showed them how to squeeze the icing out of the little tubes and to sprinkle the candy décor on top. I hid smiles when the younger ones dumped as much decoration as possible on each cookie while the older ones were more thoughtful about their designs.

I relaxed, my memories fading as I saw only smiles and merry faces, as it should be for an event like this. Until Patrick came in, holding two giant poinsettias, so huge, he staggered under their weight. Hell. I kept my attention on the children at the cookie station, which wasn't hard, as I wiped hands, offered decorating advice and tried to keep the mess down to a minimum.

This would pass and within a few weeks, I'd be able to look at him as just another business owner.

Fifteen minutes later, the caterers pulled the tops off the warmed trays of foods and families formed the buffet line, exclaiming over the variety of foods. It definitely looked better than hamburgers and pizza, but there were enough plain options that even the pickiest eater should be able to find something. Hanging back with the other volunteers and waiting until the families had gotten their food, I did a quick tidy of the cookie decorating table, filling a trash bag with broken cookies, discarded decorations and wet-wipes.

"Let me help," said a voice as I tied up the garbage bag and prepared to do a run to the dumpsters. "It's cold out there and you'll slip in your heels."

"No thank you," I said to Patrick, hefting the bag. I'd actually worn lower heels than I normally would've for this exact reason. I didn't need his help.

But he was still standing there when I got back to the table, the other volunteers either in the buffet line or sitting down to eat.

"I'm sorry," he said, pushing his glasses up his nose. "I didn't know you were a foster kid."

"It's not like they make us wear a sign or anything."

I got into the buffet line, turning my back to him. "I'm sorry," he said again. "What I said was horrible. I wasn't thinking."

"See, that's your thing," I said, spinning around. "You weren't thinking when you ordered all the fashion dolls. You weren't thinking when you said my mom—" I looked around the room and lowered my voice. "What you said about my mom. She didn't have a choice—I was there."

He looked down at the ground, his cheeks red. "I'm so sorry. I can't imagine ... it must have been horrible."

"Yeah, been to therapy; got the pin to prove it."

"And I understand why this—" he looked around. "Is so important to you. I have nothing else other than to say I'm sorry. I wasn't thinking."

"You keep saying that. You also weren't thinking when you opened your toy store, thinking putting toys on wire racks would be a successful business plan. When will you start?"

Instead of staying in the buffet line, I stomped outside, letting the icy air cool my over-hot cheeks. I wasn't going to cry—I'd cried enough in my life about my mother and what had happened. It was in the past. And it would wreck my make-up.

Out. 1. 2. 3. 4. 5. In.

The door opened behind me and Lara stepped out, my coat in her hands. She passed it to me, and I gratefully pulled it around my shoulders. "My brother is an ass sometimes."

I laughed, a quick burst. The pain he'd brought up was always there, but old and scarred over. I wasn't interested in poking at it. Not tonight. Not when tonight was about the kids. I just needed to pull myself together enough for them.

"He told me what happened. It's no excuse, but he didn't know," Lara said, tugging on her lip. "I'm not excusing his ignorance. He was an idiot. I think it's easy to forget that every child in foster care has their own story and their own reason to be there."

I grimaced. "It's a survival tactic. Like assuming all the homeless are drug addicts, rather than individuals with their own problems that put them out on the street. It makes it easier to walk by them and do nothing. I've had lots of therapy."

"We're not doing nothing tonight. Not for the foster kids. And they're taking pictures with Santa and Daphne is poorly trying to the dinner and manage the cookie station."

I took one more deep breath in and out. "Got it. I'm needed."

"Always." Lara put her hand on my shoulder. "The kids need someone like you who knows their story to help give them nights like this. Don't let my asshole brother ruin tonight. And it's freezing out here. Come on back in."

"All right, all right, you win," I said, following her back inside. "Thanks for coming and getting me."

"Of course."

I went back to my cookie station, which in the twenty minutes I'd been outside looked like puppies had attacked it. Shooing a grateful Daphne away, I wiped away crumbs, sprinkles, and cleaned up icing smears, reorganizing the chaos before allowing the kids to keep decorating. The line for Santa was a dozen kids deep waiting to take pictures and tell him their Christmas list, and some of the teenagers were standing close to the sound system, not dancing ... but ... moving slightly. Parents chatted, got cups of coffee to go with the pies and other desserts, and seemed to have fun. I took another deep breath and pushed everything else away so I could be here and enjoy this moment.

A few hours later, after everyone had left, I helped the

other volunteers do clean-up. All the presents were gone, collected by the families to place under the tree for Christmas morning. That was the only part of the evening I didn't like; I would've loved to see the kids' faces lighting up when they opened the gifts they'd asked for. But I couldn't have everything. Lara chatted while we worked, filling up the space with forgettable but entertaining stories about her past, and failed dates she'd had. I was grateful she distracted me from my thoughts. Hopefully, I'd be tired enough to go home, enjoy a quiet glass of wine with a book, and pass out. We were four days until Christmas and things were about to get even more intense. Finishing up, I grabbed my coat and turned my apron over to Daphne, who smiled, tiredly.

"Thank you for your help," she said. "Couldn't have done this without you." She gave me a hug. "After New Year's, let's go do something. Spa day or something to celebrate."

"That sounds great," I told her. I looked for Lara to say goodbye, but she was with Patrick, her hands on her hips. I wasn't going to go over there to talk to her, not in front of Patrick. She'd understand I'd Irish Goodbyed when she saw my car was gone. And she lived with Patrick; it's not like she wouldn't be able to get home. Just in case, I sent her a quick text and got a thumbs-up in response. Feeling better, I opened the doors, snow flurries floating in, sparkling with the multi-colors in the light. Mesmerized by the beauty, I turned to watch them drift, my eyes landing on Patrick. He was gazing at me, his eyes sad. "I'm sorry," he mouthed again.

There wasn't anything to say. Leaving the building, I got into my car and drove away.

## CHAPTER 24

"Merry Christmas Eve!" Lara said a few days later, brandishing coffee and pastries from Decadent Treats.

I leaned away from the computer. Online orders had pretty much stopped, but they would pick up again as people cashed in gift cards and holiday money. I'd sold a surprising amount of gift cards this year too, which was nice now and would help with orders in January and February when things slowed down; it was rare for people to spend the exact amount of their gift cards without adding on a bit more.

"I think I've gained five pounds this month," I complained, looking at the mouth-watering homemade muffins from across the street.

"Me too. But ... Taylor across the street is pretty cute." She batted her eyelashes.

I chuckled. "That explains why you're always going over there."

"Yep—I think he's going to swing by tonight after he closes," Lara said, leaning her hip on the desk. "You ready for Christmas?"

I'd been dreading it. The idea of the day stretched out in front of me, by myself, with no one to share it with, seemed horrible. And it wasn't like I could go out to a movie or get a massage or anything; everything was closed. I would literally spend the day trapped in my house.

"Of course," I lied. "Been looking forward to it. Going to sleep, and maybe binge watch some Netflix. Rest."

Lara frowned. "Do you hear that?"

I did. Movement and ... scratching? We froze, listening. "Charles?" I called out. But he was silent too, no turning on Mariah Carey, no jingling the silver bell at the front door. Maybe he was listening too. Following the sound, I went to the back door in the storage room and cautiously opened it.

"Meow?"

"Ichabod," I scolded. "What are you doing here?"

Behind me, Lara groaned. "We've had the worst time with him getting out. We don't even know how he's doing it anymore."

I scooped the cat into my arms. His fur was damp and chilled from the snow, but he didn't seem to be cold. He'd put on more weight. Purring enthusiastically, he head-butted me. Fur flew, and I wiped my face on my shoulder. "Hell Max," I scolded. "You're not supposed to come here anymore."

"He just missed you," Lara cooed, trying to take him from my arms. Ichabod gave her the dirtiest look a cat could give, and jumped away, going to hide under the desk. "I'll text Patrick."

"He definitely can't stay here." I didn't want to deal with it, not today. He wasn't my cat. He was Patrick's. And Lara's, but more Patrick's.

"He's on his way," Lara confirmed, looking up from her phone.

Swell. "I'm going to open the store," I said. "Why don't you stay with Max—Ichabod and just let me know when he's gone."

My feelings must have come through my voice, because Lara looked up sharply. "You okay?"

"Peachy-keen," I said. "It's going to be a busy day, and then die off around two. I'm just going to get us started. Thanks for the coffee and muffin!" I wasn't sure I pulled off Christmas Eve level enthusiasm, probably achieving an insanity level instead, but it was what it was. I stepped into my overly decorated store, noting the twinkling lights, the glittering gifts, and the empty Giving Tree with the sign thanking my shoppers for their donations. My store normally gave me so much joy, but today, I just felt empty and tired. Ready for Christmas to be done and go back to whatever my normal life was. But … my normal life was being alone.

A tear slipped down my cheek, and I swiped it away. The air shifted around me, the coolness of Charles sweeping by to say hello. Instrumental Christmas music began to play. I took a deep breath. I had good friends and loved my life. It was mine, and I'd chosen it. I had a business I loved that paid the bills and allowed me some financial independence. This was just an awful moment. I heard the back door open and Patrick and Lara's voice trying to coax Ichabod back out from under the desk. I went over to the front counter, ignoring them and getting the store ready for the day. Like every day this month, I could see people in their cars, waiting in front of the store for us to open.

With a whoosh of cool air, the door between the store and back room gaped and Ichabod bolted into the store, heading underneath the 70s dollhouse display. "Damn-it Charles," I hissed. "I have to open in five minutes!" Patrick and Lara ran into the store—Patrick with a box, Lara with a broom. Ichabod gave a growly hiss. "Oh hell," I said. I got down on my hands and knees in front of the display. "You two step back," I ordered, not in the mood to be nice. "Here kitty, kitty," I stretched out my hand and waggling the fingers. "Come on, baby—I gotta open."

With a prrrtttt of curiosity, Ichabod sauntered out. I scooped him up, cuddling while he purred and head-butted me. "Good kitty," I said. "Okay, but it's time to go home. Want me to put him in your car?" I asked Patrick, not looking at him.

"Sure. I'll leave him in the backseat. It's only a few miles back to the house," Patrick said, putting the box down. "I parked in front of your store."

Lara followed, unlocking the door and waving the customers waiting inside, while I went to Patrick's car, placing Ichabod in the backseat and closing the door before he could bolt again.

"Sorry," Patrick said. "I don't know how he got out this time."

I shrugged, not wanting to engage. "No big deal. I should let you get back to your shop. It's a busy day today."

"Will you..." Patrick pushed his glasses up his nose. "Consider coming to Christmas dinner? It's just me and Lara this year. Our step-siblings aren't around and it's going to be quiet. Lara says you don't have any plans. Just come, have a glass of wine—"

"I'm good," I said. "I'm looking forward to the peace and quiet tomorrow. Just me and Netflix. Gonna catch up on all the shows I've missed because I've been working so much."

Patrick nodded. "Totally understand. I'll see you around."

I turned away, trying to smile at a little girl who danced out of her car, on a Christmas high, heading into my store for the perfect Christmas moment. But instead, I just felt empty and tired.

# CHAPTER 25

"It's closing time!" I sang out at three, still trying to pretend I had the Christmas spirit, hoping that with pretending, I'd actually start feeling it. Lara gave me a high five and went to lock the front door, flipping the sign over.

I took care of the last few people in line and looked over at Lara, who was tidying displays and finishing up closing duties. "Just head out," I said. "I'll get all of this on the 26th—it'll be slower."

"Are you a take down Christmas on the 26th kind of person?" Lara asked.

"No," I confirmed. "It'll stay up until New Year's Day and then I'll put up different decorations."

"Can I help?"

I chuckled. "Of course—in fact, I'm going to do finances tomorrow, but I think if you want to work a few hours a week, even once Franklin is back, I can swing that."

Lara clapped her hands and gave me a hug. "Oh, that's the best Christmas gift of all. I've been doing so much research on dolls and dollhouses; I was hoping I could keep working here. And Patrick needs someone to stay with him, so he's not so lonely in Gramps' big house. Hopefully, I can talk him into selling it one day. But I figured I'd stick around until he was a bit more settled, and this means I don't have to look for another job."

There was a knock at the front door, and I turned around to tell whoever it was we were closed. But Lara waved, holding up one finger to show one minute. "That's Taylor. We're going out for a quick drink before Christmas. We'll see what happens. But he's fun to hang out with."

"Have an amazing time," I said, giving her a hug. "And Merry Christmas."

"Merry Christmas," she said. "If you change your mind about tomorrow—"

"I won't."

She smiled, a side-ways grin that reminded me of her brother. "If you do, just send me a text. We'd love to have you."

"Thanks," I said. She swung open the front door with the front bell jingling and together she and Taylor headed down the street. I sighed. Here we go with spending Christmas Eve and Christmas day alone.

I turned around, counting cash and getting the deposit together. I could swing by the bank before heading home. There was a knock on the front door. "Sorry! We're closed!" I called, not looking up.

The knock came again, and Charles rang the silver bell. Oh hell. We weren't doing this again. I wasn't going to open the door just because my ghost told me to. Even though it had brought me Lara, it had also brought me Patrick. Though Lara was definitely more valuable than Patrick had been. The knock came again, more insistent, followed by a rattle of the doorknob.

The silver bell rang out, dropping off the doorknob and sliding across the glittery concrete to my feet, jingling the entire time. Wow, that was new. "Fine," I muttered. "You win," I called out, louder, stepping over the bell that continued to jingle. "I'll just do whatever my ghost wants me to do—that doesn't sound insane, not at all!"

I strode to the front door, twisting the lock and swinging it open. "I'm sorry—" I started to say and froze. "Luke!" I shouted.

## CHAPTER 26

"I thought you couldn't make it," I said, my heart filling with joy as I stared at my son. "I thought I'd spend Christmas alone." A sob escaped, surprising me with its intensity. I'd been dreading the next day so much.

"I managed to get a few days off work," Luke said, wrapping me into a hug while I breathed deep, trying to get control. "We're all here." He stepped out of the way, and I gave hugs and kisses to Ivy and Tara.

"I'm so glad you all came!"

"Good surprise?" Tara asked, shivering a bit in the cold. Luke was over six feet tall, a taller version of me with the same black hair and blue eyes I had. He'd married a beautiful woman with honey-blonde hair and pale blue eyes. And she barely topped five feet, making them look a little comical when they stood together.

"Perfect surprise," I said. "Come on in!" As we walked through my store, I looked over my shoulder at Ivy. At eight-years-old, she wasn't a doll-loving girl—she preferred science projects—but her big brown eyes were bright as she took in the multi-colored chandelier, the murals of fantasy creatures on the walls, the twinkling lights, the now empty Giving Tree, and the multitude of dolls, doll clothes, and dollhouses.

"Your store is amazing," she said.

"Thank you. And I'm so sorry, but I shipped your presents to your house, so I won't have anything under the tree for you." I didn't know if she still believed in Santa. I'd have to find out—hopefully Luke and Tara had something figured out if so. "Is there anything here you might be interested in? I know you don't like dolls, but let me—"

She smiled and shook her head. I adored this eight-year-old, knowing what she wanted, and not willing to pretend to make others happy.

"We got it covered," Tara said. "Don't worry." Luke gave me a thumbs up and I relaxed.

"Okay," I said. "I'm done here. Let's head to the house and get you all settled in the guest room."

I opened the front door to find a woman on the doorstep. "Oh, thank goodness you're still open," she said, her brown hair sticking up crazily under a rainbow beanie covered in dog hair.

"Well, actually—"

"I'm so stressed out. None of my presents for my fiancé's daughter came in, and I really wanted her to have a good Christmas. And then my dog jumped on the table to steal cookies and dumped a container of milk all over the wrapping paper I had. And of course, this whole mess is totally my fault because work was kicking my butt and I delayed buying stuff ... and now I'm here. And please tell me you're still open."

"Of course we are," Ivy said, stepping aside and looking

up at me with big puppy-dog eyes, pleading for me to help this woman.

"Ivy!" Tara hissed.

"No, it's okay," I said. I looked at my granddaughter, perhaps not in blood, but in every other way that mattered. My granddaughter. Never thought I'd have an eight-year-old granddaughter when I was forty, but life was funny that way. "Want to help her make the perfect Christmas?"

"Yes!" Ivy said, jumping up and high fiving me.

"Come on in," I told the woman. "What does your fiancé's daughter like?"

Ivy helped the woman pick out the perfect gift, which turned out to be a giant dollhouse kit. "This is so cool," Ivy said, inspecting the front of the box. "You can build this?"

"Yep," I confirmed. "Harder than Legos, but you can paint everything how you want, move around the furniture, put up wallpaper, and play with it."

"That sounds like fun. I could paint it like a rainbow?"

"Of course."

"Oh! I know," Ivy said with a snap of her fingers. "Like a haunted house! All black wallpaper and cobwebs in the corners. And a coffin room instead of a dining room."

Tara laughed and the woman we were helping gave her a funny look. "She's like Wednesday Addams," Tara said, putting her arm around her daughter and looking at me, worry twisting pretty eyes.

This was too perfect! I had Christmas, and it seemed like Ivy had Halloween. I made a note to collect one of the beginner dollhouse kits off a shelf and wrap it for her to put under the tree for tomorrow morning. Maybe we could build it together on Christmas day.

Ten minutes later, Luke was following me in his rental car

back to my house. The next few hours passed in a flurry of activity as I got the guest room ready, bought groceries, and snagged some last-minute presents to have under the tree.

Christmas morning began with Ivy waking up early to tear into her presents. Luke and Tara had brought gifts for Ivy, enough so she had things to unwrap, and the day unrolled in perfect relaxation and joy as we played games and ate until our stomachs hurt.

Lara texted again to repeat her invite to Christmas dinner, and I took a break from making biscuits for Christmas dinner to respond with a picture of my family under the decorated tree, Ivy wearing Christmas pajamas.

> Luke came? Thought he couldn't!

> They came to surprise me.

> Best Christmas present ever! Take lots of pics and I can't wait to meet them.

For a minute, I thought about inviting her over for Christmas dinner. There was plenty of food, and it would be great to see her. But I couldn't invite her and not Patrick. And I wasn't sure I wanted to see him. Could I get past what he'd said about my mother and others like her? I wasn't sure I could. But it was Christmas, and Christmas was about forgiveness. And big holiday dinners with friends and family. It was just the two of them; they must miss their grandfather tremendously.

Hell. What was I supposed to do? I wanted to see Lara, but not Patrick. Or did I? He had been very apologetic—multiple times. And his mistake had been ignorance, not meanness. Many people made comments like he had about homeless people. And yes, even about foster kids. Education was the key, not condemnation. But I was still mad, no matter how I thought about it. I went back to making biscuits.

A knock echoed from the front door. "I got it," Luke called as he swung open the door. "Mom!" he yelled. "Someone for you."

Of course it was; it wasn't like anyone else knew Luke and his family were here. I wiped my doughy hands on a dishtowel and went to the front door. Patrick stood there, snow floating down to coat his hair, shivering a bit. A cat carrier was at his feet with a giant red bow on it.

"Hi," I said. "What's going on?"

"I have a present for you," Patrick said.

I looked down at the cat carrier. "Okay?"

"It's Ichabod. That damn cat got out again, and I found him in the alley behind your store. He's miserable without you. You're the only one who can pick him up without getting scratched, the only one he'll purr to. I can't even get him to eat after I picked him up yesterday. It's like he's starving himself. You're his human; I'm not. And you should have him."

"What's this?" Ivy said, opening the door and squatting in front of the carrier. "It's a cat!" She stuck her fingers into the little holes. "He's rubbing up against me," she confirmed with a giggle. "He's so soft! Can we let him in?"

I wasn't prepared for a cat. I didn't have a litter box, or food, or a bed. Or—

"I have all the stuff you need. If he's not happy, I'll take him back," Patrick said. "But I think he'll be happier with you than with me. And it's Christmas, and you'd seemed so sad when I told you he was mine."

I looked down at Ivy. "Please," Ivy said, putting her hands together in a praying pose to beg.

I couldn't say no to her. Not on Christmas day. "Okay," I said. "Let's try this."

Ivy brought the carrier in and opened it. Ichabod pranced out, rubbing up against her legs, and purring like mad, head butting her. Ivy giggled, and I picked up the cat. He curled into the space between my head and shoulder, his purrs echoing through my body. We stayed like that for a few minutes, then Ivy asked to hold the cat. I settled him in her arms, and he stayed before hopping down to explore his new home. Ivy followed him with a giggle, Luke and Tara going after them to make sure they didn't break anything.

I turned back to thank Patrick. He'd gone out to his car and was setting a cardboard box on the porch. I was still mad, but he'd just made my granddaughter's Christmas, and that had to count.

"I know giving you Ichabod doesn't make up for what I said. Nothing will. I said ... what I said about parents ... well ... God, I can't even repeat it, it was so horrible." He pushed his glasses up his nose. "But it was out of ignorance and stupidity. And I'm sorry."

He turned to go.

"Wait, come back," I called, my heart melting. It was Christmas, after all. "Why don't you and Lara come over for Christmas dinner? I was just thinking about how it's just the two of you at your Gramps' place and how we have all this food. The more the merrier for Christmas. Why don't you two move your Christmas dinner over here?"

Patrick's eyes lit up. "Are you sure?"

Ichabod pranced over, rubbing against my legs while Ivy squatted at my feet to pet him. Life was too short to hold grudges. "I'm sure," I said. "Come in for Christmas dinner! I'll call Lara."

He stepped out of the cold and into my warm house, introducing himself to my family.

# EPILOGUE

*P*atrick wiped paint from my forehead, swiping his finger on his paint-stained shirt. "Thank you," I said, giving him a kiss on the cheek.

"The paint looked cute on you, though," Patrick said. "Just didn't want you to get it in your hair."

I leaned back to examine the stripes of paint on the plaster walls I'd done in his store. Patrick had great plans for how to turn his place into the fun, sleek, and modern store he envisioned, including more robotics, and more fun for the children who liked science and physics. But he lacked the money at this point to make it happen.

However, paint was cheap. And with a new paint job, a few easy displays, and a repair job on The Claw (formally Mr. ToyDrop) he'd be turning a greater profit than he had during Christmas time in just a few months, I was predicting.

"What do you think?" I asked, pointing at the wall I'd just painted with yellow, blue and black stripes.

"I like it," he said, not looking at the wall, but instead

cupping his hand under my chin to pull me close for a kiss. His hands roved to my butt, and I slapped his hand away.

"Later," I said with mock frustration. "You're going to get paint everywhere."

"Too late," he laughed, pushing his paint-speckled glasses up his nose. He pressed his forehead to mine for a quick moment, a loving gesture I was still getting used to. We'd been officially dating for three months now, and it was hard to believe I'd been so frustrated with him, hard to believe I'd misunderstood him so much. While we'd been on separate sides of the toy debate, we were so similar with our other interests of travel, movies, and books, there was always plenty to talk about.

I looked at the picture of his grandfather we'd hung behind the cash register. It seemed important to keep the man whose dream this had been centered in the store. Like always, I wondered if he'd be proud of his grandson; I thought so, but it was hard to know. No ghosts in this store, at least not that we'd discovered.

"Come on," I said. "Let's get cleaned up. I need to go help Franklin close my store."

"Mmmmm..." Patrick's hand went back to my butt. "I like the idea of a shower at my house, both of us together."

I laughed and pulled him in for a kiss. Between the two of us, with his soon-to-be sleek and modern store and with my store of whimsy and imagination, we'd dominate the toy market in this town.

# AUTHOR'S NOTE

And that's a wrap, pun intended. I've always wanted to do a Christmas romance, play with the clichés and tropes and write a fun little holiday story; something that would help people get into the Christmas mood. And here it is: *Wrapping Paper Rivals*. Thank you for picking it up and giving it a go!

As always, I work little Easter Eggs into my stories. Growing up, my mother and I collected Madame Alexander dolls, going to the doll fairs and oohing and awwing over the beautiful outfits. I collected the Presidential Wives and brides from different countries, among others. We both still have our collections, too precious to give away or sell, and my mother still has several from when she was younger. I also have always enjoyed dollhouses and miniatures and built my own dollhouse at one point. My enjoyment probably has something to do with how much I like creating worlds. One day, I'd love to build some miniatures of the Warehouse from my Warehouse Dreams series (it's a good series—pick it up!). Additionally, it's cheaper to decorate a dollhouse, and change out things like furniture, wallpaper

## AUTHOR'S NOTE

and flooring than it is on a real house. I've hated construction every time I've had to do it in my real house, and it's so expensive!

But my affection for dolls and dollhouses isn't the only Easter Egg in this book–my son Connor had a stuffed koala named Ratty that he adored and went everywhere with him. My sons both enjoyed collecting stuffed animals from the various zoos and aquariums we visited, playing with them for weeks afterwards.

Of course, I can't write books without my team, and for this one, Margaret and Stephanie were both wonderful beta readers with Margaret catching a big error that hopefully was resolved. I also have the Sages, Morrigan and Molly, as always, to thank for being wonderful cheerleaders. And if you want to see some fun, head over to the Semi-Sages of the Pages Discord channel. There was one evening when several members and I giggled as we tried to come up with the tagline for the cover. Warning: there's a lot of innuendo in those taglines that weren't appropriate for this book. But we sure laughed a lot.

Again, thank you for picking up this book and getting this far. Reviews are invaluable, especially for authors like me, so please consider leaving a review anywhere you think is appropriate.

And whether or not it's the holiday time for you, Merry Christmas to you and your family. I hope it's a magical time of year for you and yours.

# ABOUT THE AUTHOR

Theresa Halvorsen can't seem to pick a genre to write in and this is her second contemporary romance. In addition to being an author, she's also a publisher, editor, and YouTuber. She's overly-caffeinated and at times, wine-soaked. The author of multiple cross-genre works, including Warehouse Dreams, Lost Aboard and River City Widows, Theresa wonders what sleep is. She's the owner of No Bad Books Press and one of the hosts of the popular YouTube channel, the Semi-Sages of the Pages. In whatever free time is left, (ha!) Theresa enjoys board games, concerts, geeky conventions, and reading. Her life goal is to give "Oh-My-Gosh-This-Book-Is-So-Good!" happiness to her readers. She lives in Temecula with her husband, her adult children, their partners (she has no idea who actually lives in her house and who's just visiting) and many pets. Find her on social media —she's on all of them or send an email to halvorsentheresa@gmail.com to say hi. She'd love to hear from you.

# OTHER BOOKS BY THE AUTHOR

### Warehouse Dreams

Meet Kendle, a teacher trying to keep her supernatural students from blowing up the school. And this year, a hot new teacher has joined the team. And she can't stand him.

### Lying, Baking & Surfing

Sabrina and Jonathan meet while pretending to be someone else. She doesn't actually own a yoga studio and he's not actually a surf instructor. Instead, they're burnt out professionals, hoping for a different life.But how far will they go to keep the illusion alive when they fall in love?

### Lost Aboard

The authors interviewed cast, crew, and volunteers to get their true ghost stories from aboard the Star of India. But

OTHER BOOKS BY THE AUTHOR

they didn't stop there—they interspersed them with stories from the log-books too. Enjoy this spooky read!

### River City Widows

Tasia is a young window whose stepdaughter brings an ouija board home from college. The use of it unlocks mysteries and from the widow who owned the house previously.

### Tiny Gateways

This collection of portal short stories was inspired because Theresa has yet to fall into a portal to a new world. One day, she hopes it'll happen.

Made in the USA
Middletown, DE
11 December 2024

66721959R00117